SEARCHING FOR
SARA

JAMES R. FRAZEE

Searching for Sara
Copyright © 2018 by James R. Frazee

FICTION

The Mosquito Bites (2018)

NONFICTION

Beginning Bridge by the Numbers (2014)

Quick and Healthy Recipes from the Store (2014)

Library of Congress Control Number: 2020911753
ISBN-13:   Paperback: 978-1-64674-125-0
                PDF: 978-1-64674-132-8
                ePub: 978-1-64674-126-7
                Kindle: 978-1-64674-133-5

Printed in the United States of America

LitFire LLC
1-800-511-9787
www.litfirepublishing.com
order@litfirepublishing.com

Contents

Dedication

To my brothers and sister; my two older brothers, Terry and Bob, who led the way for my growth, my sister Shannon, who had to grow up before her time; and my youngest brother, Tom, who grew into a young man on his own. No matter how spread out we are, we will always be family.

Books by James R. Frazee

FICTION

Searching for Sara (2020)

Searching for Sara is a work of fiction. Names, characters, locations, and incidents are the result of the author's imagination and used as a fiction. Any resemblance to actual events, locations, or persons, living or dead, is entirely coincidental.

The Mosquito Bites (2018)

The Mosquito Bites is a work of fiction. Names, characters, locations, and incidents are the result of the author's imagination and used as a fiction. Any resemblance to actual events, locations, or persons, living or dead, is entirely coincidental.

NONFICTION

Beginning Bridge by the Numbers (2017)

Quick and Healthy Recipes from the Store (2014)

WEBSITE
http://JamesFrazeeBooks.com

Preface

In **The Mosquito Bites**, Alex and Leslie put their lives in danger when they exposed a large corporation that was about to introduce a dangerous new pesticide into the environment. The product would make millions for a corporation in financial trouble, but it also caused a biological change in nature that could cause the demise of humanity over time. Three other people who had previously discovered the truth about this product had suddenly died. This first book takes a closer look at the irresponsibility and even fatal manufacturing of products in pursuit of large bonuses for upper management and increased bottom-line result for a company. When it comes to profit over safety, profit often wins.

Searching for Sara starts with the trial of the corporate executives responsible for the manufacture of a new product dangerous to the environment, and their involvement in the deaths of three employees. Alex and Leslie are being stalked by a man whose sole purpose is to eliminate them because of their part in his incarceration.

A dark secret in Leslie's early years resurfaces that leads Alex and Leslie on a new path. Alex helps Leslie face this secret and find some closure. At the same time, they must make sure the stalker does not find them. These two events put a real strain on their relationship.

Will they survive either or both challenges, or will he fail and just become another statistic? Will Leslie need to go on without Alex and see where it takes her?

Chapter 1

Home! It sure feels good Alex thought as he stood outside the twelve-story apartment building looking up at the structure. He could see the windows of his apartment on the sixth floor. An apartment he had spent more time away from, then actually being there. Maybe he can get back to a normal life now that he is home. As he started up the steps to the entrance of the building, the doorman was already there holding the door open for him.

"Good Morning Dr. Gregory. Welcome back" the doorman remarked.

"Good Morning Stanley. It is good to be back."

Alex entered the lobby and headed to the back stairs. He could have taken the elevator, but he wanted to avoid any questions from the doorman about his whereabouts the past several weeks. The activity at Sterling Chemicals, a company he where he just started working about two month ago, has been in the news almost daily. As he reached the door to the stairwell, he saw the Superintendent coming up from the basement.

"Hello Dr. Gregory. Good to see you back."

The Super was always fixing something in this one hundred year old building. It is one of pre-war buildings that still exists on the Upper West Side of Manhattan. Large rooms with eleven-foot ceilings, classic crown moldings and large windows streaming light into all the rooms characterizes these old buildings. So many of the pre-war buildings are being torn down and replaced with steel and glass apartments with low ceilings and no character. Some people call that progress. His building has been landmarked, so it will can not be replaced with a new building.

"It is good to be back. Did anything exciting happen while I was gone?" Alex asked the Super as he started up the stairs. *Why did he ask that question…it would only lead to a conversation?* Alex continued up the stairs hoping to avoid any more questions from the Super.

"Nothing to report here. There was a lot of excitement at the company where you work. The papers and TV have been reporting it for weeks. But I'm sure you know all about that."

Alex gave a shrug to the Super as he turned the corner of stairwell heading to the sixth floor.

Yes, I know a lot about what happened at my company; more than I wish Alex thought as he continued up the stairs. He opened the door to the sixth-floor landing and headed to Apartment 6C.

He unlocked his apartment door, closing and locking it behind him. He leaned back against it and looked around as if he were seeing the place for the first time. *I'm finally home* he thought. Everything was as he had left it, a box of corn flakes sitting on the coffee table and his running shorts lying on the floor in the middle of the room.

He moved to the bedroom to unpack the few items he had a chance to take with him, all stuffed in a knapsack. A polo shirt was draped over the back of a chair and his running shoes at the foot of his unmade bed where he had left them. Yup, this is home...just as I left it.

Has it only been three weeks since I was here? he thought to himself as he opened his knapsack and dumped the contents on the bed. *It seemed much longer than that.* He stripped off his clothes and headed to take a shower. He couldn't wait to feel the warm water spray on his body. He stepped into the tub and stood there for a long time with his eyes closes letting the water run down his body.

His solitude was broken by the ringing of his phone. It was his land line phone, not his cell phone. He wondered why he still had a land phone. Every time he thought about canceling the service, he changed his mind, believing he needed it for emergency purposes.

They would just have to wait. Leave a message. I'll call back when I get out of the shower. Probably Leslie or his mom he thought to himself. He had only moved in about two months ago and not many people had the land line number. The only other people who had that number was Human Resources and his boss at work.

He closed his eyes again and just enjoyed the water flowing over his body. The phone rang again, and the trance was broken. He waited for the click of the recorder. No click, no message. Then he realized that he hadn't hear a recording from the first phone call either. Who would call and not leave a message? Probably one of those Robo-callers that are popping up all over the place, tempting people to get a credit card, or people trying to sell solar energy, or a free security system. They never leave messages but keep calling, repeatedly all from different numbers.

When is someone going to come up with a way to stop those calls? They are so annoying.

After a few minutes of solitude, he opened his eyes, reached for the faucet, and turned off the water. He felt so much better. Stepping out of the shower he grabbed a towel to dry himself, starting with his hair working down to his feet. Putting the towel around his waist he turned and saw his reflection in the full-length mirror on the back of the bathroom door. He ran his fingers through his strawberry-blond hair pushing it in place. He needed to have it cut.

Alex stood a little over six feet tall. He was worried that he might have put on a few pounds from the good treatment he got from Leslie's parents while living with them the pass three weeks. Every meal was full of calories, but too good to pass. His reflection showed a well-defined, smooth chest, a flat stomach, and muscular legs. A strong square chin, straight teeth, sky-blue eyes, perfect nose, and long dark eyelashes rounded out his face. He had not been to the gym for a month to work out, but his reflection showed no change in his body, still slim and trim. He did however look forward to starting his gym routine tomorrow. There was a gym only a block from his apartment he joined as soon as he moved to New York. He would run over early in the morning in his workout clothes and run back to shower before heading to work.

Just then his cell phone rang. *I sure am popular* he thought to himself as he headed to the living room. He saw the name on the phone and a smile came over his face.

"I see you got home okay" came a voice from the phone as soon as he picked it up and put it to his ear. No time to even say hello.

"Hi Leslie. Yes, I'm here. The place is exactly like I left it. Although it was great being with you and your parents, it is good to be home."

"I know what you mean. I just finished unpacking and putting things away. It will be good to sleep in my own bed tonight and try to get back to a normal life. My father has already called me twice to see if I am okay."

"That's what parents do. They just want to know that you are safe and happy. They will probably still worry about you when you are old and in a rocking chair."

There was a pause, as if she wasn't sure what to say. He waited but no response.

"Is something bothering you Leslie? You went silent."

"Are you worried about tomorrow" she asked?

"Not worried, but it is going to be different going into the office after being gone for more than a month. Especially since we just started working there. We've been away from the office almost as long as we've been there. I wonder if they have given my desk to someone else." Alex said trying to lighten the situation.

"I'm sure it is still there, just as you left it. However, I have the same trepidations about my position."

"Well, we will see tomorrow. Only one of two things can happen; they can tell us to pack up and leave or welcome us back. It could be the shortest career in history. The lady or the tiger. But it is time to find out."

"Two options. I hope it is the one I want. Putting it off is not going to make it any easier or less strenuous."

Alex continued "With what has happened at work, the company has taken a big hit. I've been watching the stock price…not good. People at work are probably worried about a layoff to help the bottom line. We may be one of the unlucky ones. But on the bright side, I heard that unemployment benefits in New York are good."

"You always find the bright side in everything. That is one characteristic I like in you."

"Is that the only one?"

Alex expected a response from Leslie. Again, there was silence, so Alex added "How are you really feeling about going back?"

"Like you, it is going to be strange. There were only seven of us on the entire executive floor when I left. Three of them have been indicted, one is dead. That leaves me, Barb the receptionist and one Vice President. The only one that I am sure was not affected by what we uncovered is Barb. She may be the only one there. I may also be packing within minutes after arriving. Not much of a career."

"Leslie, you will be okay. Who wouldn't want you working for them?"

"You always say the sweetest things."

4

"Well, it's true. You know what we did was right. Just hold your head up and walk in as if you hadn't been gone. I bet you will be received with open arms."

"I hope you are right, but I still have concerns. If I am welcomed back, there aren't many arms there to welcome me. I may have to find you and have you put your arms around me." That put a smile on Alex's face.

"That means they will have to make you a Vice President."

"No thank you...not my cup of tea".

"How about I meet you outside the building tomorrow at 8:45 and we can walk in together?" Alex asked. "And if you want, I'll go up with you to your office."

"That sounds good. I'll meet you in the morning in front of the building on the 46th street entrance. But I need to go up to my work area on my own. And you need to go to your area. Thanks for the offer though."

"I'll be there waiting for you. Don't worry, you will be fine."

"Thanks Alex. Time for me to get something to eat and relax."

"Are you okay now" he asked? "Do you want me to come over?"

"No, I'm fine. I need to go to the grocery store and go through my mail. My cupboards are like Old Mother Hubbard's...bare. Although I am tempted to have you come over, I think we both need to get a good night's rest. And if you were here, I don't think that would happen. I'll see you tomorrow, 8:45."

"Bye Leslie. I'm sure everything in my fridge is sour or moldy. I think I will just order in and shop tomorrow. I might even have a free day tomorrow."

"You are too funny. Bye Alex. Thank you for being you."

"I'm the winner here Leslie. And thanks again to your parents for letting me stay with them.

"Thanks Alex. Let's talk tonight before we go to bed."

"I can't wait." Alex responded and he heard her phone disconnect.

As Alex put the phone down, the events of the last two months went through his head, all leading to the position he is in now; does he or does he not have a job...his first job out of college. That won't look good on a resume. He will find out tomorrow.

I'll have to look up the number for unemployment benefits before tomorrow.

Chapter 2

*A*lex remembered the first time he saw Leslie. It was only about two months ago, but he felt that he has known her for years. The last two months had been both exciting and terrifying. With everything they had been through, it was hard to keep track of the days and how long they had been anywhere.

All new employees had to report to a conference room for orientation on their first day. He was almost late because of delays in the subway at his stop. That was no way to start a new job…walking in late.

He got to the subway platform forty-five minutes before he was to report to work; enough time to give him a fifteen minutes window of time. He had practiced that run twice so not to be late on his first day. Even with his practice runs, he was almost late.'

The subway system in New York was perfect for him. It was two blocks from his apartment to the underground station, and then only two subway stops, followed by a four block walk this office. His practice runs took about thirty minutes, door to door.

He stood on the subway with all the early morning commuters looking down the track waiting for the train lights to appear around the curve into the station. More people continued to arrive at the platform, all looking for a space to stand, waiting for the train to arrive.

He found himself packed shoulder to shoulder with other people waiting for the same subway.

The subway finally arrived, the doors opened, and he pushed his way in. Being rush hour the subway was full. All the seats were occupied so he had to stand. People were packed in like sardines. The doors closed and the train didn't move. Then an announcement came over the speakers stating that they are being delayed due to 'activity on the track'. Right away people started complaining about the service and they would be late for work.

He had read about the New York subways, but now he was experiencing it. Being his first-time during rush hour his adrenaline was high. He looked around and found a diversity of people; tall, short, some in suits, others in T-shirts and shorts, all ethnic groups. Some riders were trying to read a book, some listening to music or playing games on their iPhones, some even trying to sleep. Very few were talking…everyone was in their own world, no one making eye contact. Ten minutes later the train started down the track. He still had a five-minute cushion of time.

Those standing were pushed against each other, swaying in unison as the train sped down the track to the next stop. He was on an express train so only had two stops and then he got off at Time Square. An elderly woman with a cane pushed up against him. No one offered to give up their seat for her.

At the first stop on seventy-second street, few people left the train car and more pushed their way in, everyone trying to find their space. More sardines…

The train took off for the next stop where Alex would get off and get some fresh air. It was a major stop right in the center of the city with lots of office buildings in the area. There would be a mass exit off the train at that stop. As the train entered the station everyone turned toward the doors, ready to push their way out. The doors opened everyone rushed out of the subway cars, up the stairs from the platform, phones out checking messages heading to their next destination. This was what Alex had to look forward to doing every morning on his way to work.

Once he was out of the subway, he joined the mass of workers heading to work, everyone walking at the same pace while checking their text messages. These were true New Yorkers He headed to Sterling Chemicals located at Park Avenue and 46th street. It was four blocks to the building, and he wanted to make up lost time due to the delay. He rushed into the lobby of the building, signed in at the security desk and took the elevator to the twelfth floor, entering the conference room five minutes before the scheduled start time.

Scanning the table for an empty chair, his eyes stopped on a woman sitting on the other side of the table. She sat straight up, her back not even touching the back of the chair, with her hands in her lap. She glanced his way, and he thought he saw a slight smile as their eyes met. He just stood there and stared back for a moment.

He was sure he had never seen a woman so beautiful and one who looked so confident at the same time. Just then another person entered the room behind him. Alex quickly moved to the empty chair next to the woman before anyone else sat there. He tried to appear as if he knew what he was doing, even though he was nervous and excited at the same time.

He quickly sat down, placing his knapsack on the floor next to his chair. He felt like a schoolboy with his first crush.

"Hi, I'm Alex Gregory," he introduced himself.

"Hi, I'm Leslie Sherwood" she responded.

"I guess we are both new."

From that day on, whenever he heard her name or thought of her, a good feeling overtook his body. He learned that she would be working on the executive floor as an Administrative Assistant to a Senior Vice President.

Two months had passed since that first meeting and she had become a major factor in his life. They saw each other almost daily at work and even dated several times outside of work. They were both instantly attracted to each other. As he sat there thinking about that moment, the same feeling he had when he saw her the first day came over him. He didn't want that feeling to ever go away. But there was also the dark side of their new adventure.

He was still wrapped in a towel after a shower, holding the phone thinking of Leslie and how they met.

He put the phone done and started back to the bedroom to get dressed for the workday. As soon as he put the phone down it rang again. Assuming it was Leslie or his mom, he picked it up immediately rather than letting it go to voice mail.

"Hello"

"Is this Alex Gregory?"

"Yes, it is. Who is this?" he asked, not recognizing the voice.

"My name is Alan Peters. I'm a free-lance reporter here in New York. I understand you were responsible for exposing the danger of the new pesticide being marketed by Sterling Chemicals where two executives have been arrested. Do you have anything to add?"

"I'm sorry, I don't know anything about that" Alex responded and hung up. *That was strange,* he thought to himself. *How did they find me? My name was never mentioned anywhere in the newspapers or mentioned on the TV news reports. There was supposed to have been a gag order to the press.*

He headed to the kitchen to see what he had in the refrigerator that was still good.

His land line phone rang again. Without thinking he answered.

"Hello?"

"Alex Gregory?"

"Yes."

"My name is Joy Tish. I'm writing an article about the upcoming trial for..."

Alex hung up the phone. Almost immediately it rang again. He let it go to his answering machine. The ringing eventually stopped, and he heard the click of the answering machine, but no message was left. He looked at the machine and noticed that he had 50 messages waiting, the maximum number the machine could hold. There was no room for anyone to leave a message. That is why the callers from this morning didn't leave a message.

He pushed the button on the recorder...

"This is Tom Barton from the Los Angeles Times. I would like to talk to you about the Sterling Chemicals' trial. Pease call me back at..." Alex hit the delete button.

He spent the next thirty minutes listening to the recorded messages, deleting all the messages from people asking about the upcoming trial. When he was finished there were only three messages left, all from his mom.

He felt a chill go through him. How did they get his name and number? No one knew he was the one responsible for uncovering the Sterling secrets. He had a messenger deliver the incriminating documents about Sterling to the police so no would be able to track the documents back to him.

Was it the courier who let his name leak? And how did they know that he was home? He had been staying with Leslie's parents for several weeks. Is he being watched?

Questions kept popping into his head. Instinctively he went to the window to see if he noticed anyone watching the building.

Isn't that what they do in the movies?

Hard to tell from way up here.

Just then the phone rang again. He heard the answering machine click on." This is Peter Pushing from the Chicago Tribune. I'd appreciate it if…." Alex reached down and unplugged the phone base from the wall.

He took out his cell phone and checked to see if there were any messages. Thank God there weren't any.

Apparently only one reporter has found his cell phone number.

He needed to calm down. He couldn't call Leslie. It would only upset her. *Was she also getting calls from reporters* he thought? He dialed his home number in Minnesota on his cell phone.

"Hi Mom, how are you doing?"

"Oh Alex, I have been so worried about you. I tried calling you, but it always went to the answering machine. And then I got the message that your machine was full. And I couldn't find your cell phone number. The trouble at Sterling Chemicals has been all over the news here. And when I couldn't get hold of you, I just worried since I know you work there. Is everything okay?"

Alex listened as she quickly rattled off one question after the other. He knew she needed to get that out.

Alex had been calling his mom from his cell phone since he went into hiding and didn't tell her anything about the Sterling case for fear she would worry. She found out anyway and he was right, she was worried.

"I'm sorry mom. So much has been going on here that I just forgot to call you. Starting a new job takes a lot of time and effort. I didn't realize how much I had to learn. I've been working late every night to learn the ropes. Also, I went on a business trip to the companies' research farm in North Carolina so lost a week there. I have only been working here a little over two months, but it feels much longer. And finding and moving into my first apartment took up any free time I had. I'm all moved in and have time now to relax and catch up on what is happening in the world around me."

It never dawned on him that the events at Sterling would be on the news back in Minnesota.

"I have nothing to do with what is happening at Sterling, I just work there" he continued. "Like you I only know what is reported in the newspaper and on TV" he lied. I'm surprised it even got on the news back there."

"I was just worried, that's all. You are so far away and when I couldn't get in touch with you...well all types of things went through my head."

"Mom, you have nothing to worry about. The papers exaggerate the truth to sell papers. I'm an adult now and can take care of myself."

He didn't like lying to his parents, even if to protect them. He was also glad that his name and involvement in the Sterling incident had never been leaked to the news. That would really put his mom over the edge. But then again, if reporters knew to call him why didn't his name appear in the news articles? The gag order?

"Alex, I'm your mother. I will always worry about you. Your father keeps telling me you will be okay, but I still worry. I'm so glad you answered when I called. I might be able to sleep tonight."

"I'm back home now in my own apartment."

"What do you mean 'back home.'? Where have you been?"

"I told you I was on a business trip for the company for a couple of days. Then I've been going to Connecticut with Leslie and staying at her home. Her parents have been very nice to me."

"Why have you been staying with them? Is something wrong with your place or is there something you aren't telling us? You couldn't find time to call me?"

There's his mom's questioning everything again.

"They had some plumbing problems in my apartment, and they had to take care of, so I had to move out" Alex lied again. "Leslie let me say with her in her spare bedroom and then on weekends went to her parent's home in Connecticut. It is so much cheaper staying with her than renting a hotel room. Especially on my salary." *Another lie.* "With all that has been going on here, I just forgot to call. I'm sorry mom."

"You should have moved back home and found a job here."

"Mom, I just couldn't turn down this opportunity and have a chance to live in New York City. Plus...be my own man."

There was a pause and then his mom added "Leslie seems important to you."

"Yes, she is mom. She is a special person. I hope you have a chance to meet her sometime when you are here. Or maybe I will invite her to Minnesota for Christmas." That just popped out of his mouth without ever thinking. Nothing had ever been discussed about her travelling with him back to Minnesota, and especially at Christmas.

"Then you will be home for Christmas. You have never brought a girl home for Christmas. She must be very special to you."

"Yes, she is mon. You will like her.'

"Are you sure you know nothing about the Sterling case I am hearing on the news?"

"Mom, there are over 5,000 people working in that building. I'm just one of them, going to work every day doing my job." Alex needed to steer her away from anything to do with Sterling Chemicals. "Just know that I am okay. You have nothing to worry about."

"You know I will always worry. You are my baby."

"I'm far from a baby mom. I'm on my own now."

"Wait until you have a child and then you will know what I am feeling."

"That won't be for a long while yet. Let me give you my cell phone number again. Call me on that number. I always have it with me" Alex said changing the subject. "My answering machine isn't working on my other phone, so I unplugged it." Another lie.

"Why don't you just come home where I can watch over you? You probably haven't been eating right."

"I need to be here mom, and I need to go to work. I have rent to pay. And don't worry about my eating. Leslie's parents took good care of me."

He wished he hadn't made that statement about Leslie's parents. That might just open another can of worms for him to explain away with more lies.

"Got a paper and pencil to take down my cell number" he quickly added.

Alex gave her the number and asked her to read it back making sure she had it correct.

"Now put that someplace where you won't lose it."

"I'm going to have it tattooed to the back of my hand" she said with the first hint of joy in her voice."

"A tattoo won't look good with your jewelry" he replied trying to end the conversation on a light level. "I'm sorry I forgot to call you. I promise I will call you every week if not more, and you call me whenever you want."

"I'm just so glad that you are all right, Alex."

They spent the next thirty minutes talking about things at home, Alex avoiding talking about work.

"I'm glad that Auntie Wilma is doing better after her fall. Give her my love. I need to go mom. The plumbing is fixed in my building. I just got home and have a lot to do before going to work tomorrow. Love you mom. Let me talk to dad for a few minutes,"

"Don't forget that you promised to call. Take care of yourself Alex. Love you."

"Hello son. Your mom has been driving me crazy worrying about you. How are you doing? Do you need anything?"

"I'm fine dad. I know mom…she worries about everything. But it is my fault for not calling. I think she is happy now. I promised to call more often."

He spent ten minutes more on the phone with his dad, again avoiding the Sterling situation.

"Hey dad, the battery on my phone is going dead and we might be cut off. Best we hang up before that happens."

"I'm going to hold you to calling us weekly as promised. And I want to know how you are doing. Promise to call?"

"Yes, I promise to call. Take care of mom, and don't worry, I am doing okay."

"Okay son. If you need anything, call. We are always here for you"

"Bye dad, love you."

Alex turned off his phone. The phone's battery was a little low so that wasn't a total lie. Even though he was an adult and on his own, he missed his parents and being home. He had been so busy that he didn't have much time to think about them. He hated having to lie to them. But this was his home now; well at least for the time being.

He went to the bedroom and got the phone charger out of his knapsack and plugged it in on the dresser. Throwing the towel over the shower door he again examined his form in the mirror. He grabbed a pair of basketball shorts from his dresser, put them on and headed to the kitchen.

Grabbing a beer from the refrigerator he returned to the living room, turned on the TV, put his feet up on the coffee table and sat back to watch the news, knowing the phone wouldn't ring again since it was unplugged. He will have to remember to plug it in tomorrow before he goes to work.

It wasn't long before news about the upcoming Sterling trial came on the screen. Alex, put the beer down so he could concentrate on what was being said.

"We have an update to the Sterling Chemicals murders. As reported earlier, several people at Sterling Chemicals have been arrested in the murder for hire of three employee. Those arrested included Tony Gianti, a Senior Vice President, and his assistant Rob Schimel. A third person, Tony Neuman, a consultant at Sterling Chemicals was also arrested. The police investigation determined that the three victims probably had information detrimental to the company and were murdered before they could expose the company secrets. Several other top executives were fired or resigned because of the cover-up. Sterling Chemical's stock dropped 20%. Charles Sterling, CEO of the company will be restructuring the company due to the current events and promises to have more hands-on contact with his employees. The company secrets were uncovered by an employee who reported it to New York Times and the New York Police. That employee's name is being withheld."

No name was mentioned, but Alex knew that they were talking about him…he was that employee. They didn't say anything about a woman helping him, so Leslie and Cindy were safe.

"We just learned that a trial date has been set for next month, with jury selection starting in two weeks. Sterling Chemicals is a major multi-national company with gross earnings of six hundred million dollars with over sixty-five thousand employees world-wide. Sterling was about to sell a new pesticide that was very harmful to the environment. This trial has all the interests of the environmentalists. We will report any new information as it becomes available. Now on to the weather…"

Alex had been following the case in the newspaper and on TV for the past month. It had hit all the local TV stations almost daily. It even reached Minnesota. Now they have the trial date set. That is probably why he is getting so many phone calls from newspapers. Someone found out that he might know something about the murders at Sterling. The more he thought about it, the more he was sure it had to be the courier who delivered his package to the newspaper and the Police Department. He hadn't told the courier what was in the package, but somehow, the courier must have linked him to the Sterling case.

I wonder if Leslie and Cindy are getting phone calls from reporters too. I can't wait until all of this is behind me.

Just then there was a knock on his door. It had to be a neighbor since anyone coming in from the outside would have rung the buzzer at the front door downstairs for him to buzz them in. Opening the door he saw a stranger standing there.

"Alex Gregory?"

"Yes."

The man handed Alex a document and a piece of paper. "You have been served. Also, please call this number on the piece of paper as soon as possible." The man turned and left, leaving Alex standing in the doorway holding the document.

Just then his cell phone rang. Picking up the phone with the charger still attached he saw that it was Leslie calling.

"Hi Leslie. Everything OK?"

"A man just appeared at my door and handed me a summons to appear in court and a number to call."

"I just had the same thing happen to me. What number did they give you?"

Leslie read off the number. It was the same number that was given to Alex.

"Let me get back to you. I'm going to call Cindy and see if she got a summons also. I'll call you right back Leslie. Don't call the number. Let me find out what is going on and I'll call you. Just hold tight. Before you hang up, have you received any phone calls from newspapers or reporters looking for a comment on the case?"

"No. Why do you ask?"

"My answering machine was filled with requests from reporters across the country asking for a statement. And three called me this morning since I got home. I wonder how they got my name. It was never published. And how did they get your name to serve you the summons. Your name was never mentioned in any of the documents. I think the delivery company is the one who gave my name out. I'm glad no one has tried to contact you."

"I'm sorry Alex. What have we gotten into?"

"Don't worry, let me call Cindy and see if she has been served and if she has been getting phone calls. I'll get right back to you"

"Be careful Alex. I'm getting that scary feeling again."

"Don't worry Leslie. We have done nothing wrong and all the bad people are locked up. I'll talk to you soon" he said and hung up to call Cindy.

Almost immediately the phone rang. The name Cindy Hudson appeared on the phone.

"Hi Cindy. I was just about to call you."

"I just got a summons to appear in court. What do I do?"

"Leslie and I just got one too. They sure had this all timed right. Let me follow up on this and I'll get back to you. Don't do anything yet and don't worry. We were in the right. Have you received any calls from reporters or anyone you didn't know asking for a comment on the upcoming trial?"

"No. Why do you ask? Have you gotten any calls? Our names were never released."

"I've gotten a few since I got home. Leslie hasn't received any either. Somehow they found me."

"Is it starting all over again?"

"Let me call the number and find out what this is all about. I'll get back to you within the hour. Don't worry; the bad guys are all locked up. Bye Cindy."

Chapter 3

"*G*ood Morning, District Attorney's office, how may I help you?" a voice answered.

"I am supposed to contact a Lisa Fisher at this number" Alex responded, referencing the name and phone number that was delivered to him this morning.

"Whom may I say is calling?"

"Alex Gregory."

"One moment please, Ms. Fisher is expecting your call."

Alex heard a click on the phone. Almost immediately someone came on the line.

"Dr. Gregory, thank you for calling me back. I am with the District Attorney's Office in Manhattan. I have been looking forward for a chance to talk with you about the Sterling Chemical case. The trial date has been set. I would like to set up a time to meet with you before that to go over your testimony?"

Go over my testimony Alex thought. Images of court room scenes from television programs stared racing through his head.

Alex had never had any contact with an attorney, especially one from the District Attorney's office. He started to sweat.

"Why do you want to talk to me?" he asked. He was sure she could hear the anxiety in his voice. He tried to be calm but was not winning that battle.

"You are the person who uncovered the conspiracy at Sterling Chemicals. It is only natural that we want to hear directly from you what you found and how you found it. It is important that we get all the facts directly from you. The documents you delivered to the police provide supporting evidence to the case. We also want to prepare you for your testimony in court."

"My testimony!" Alex exclaimed. "Why do you think I know anything?"

"This office was contacted by the police once they reviewed the documents you left with them a few weeks ago."

"What do you mean the documents I left?"

"Dr. Gregory, it didn't take us long to find the delivery man who dropped off the documents and then find you through the courier company."

Damn, it was the delivery man after all. Probably also how the reporters found out. No sense trying to hide anything anymore, especially from the law.

"You have all the documents that I provided to the police. I can't add any more to that. You know everything that I know, so why do you need to talk to me?" Alex asked again, hoping that she would agree with him. But after he made that statement, he knew it was a weak attempt to get out of talking to her.

"We need to have your direct testimony to prove the conspiracy and murder charges in the Sterling Chemicals Case. Also, during our conversation you may remember things not in the documents."

"If you found out who I was, then the press knows it also. I have been getting phone calls from reporters for a statement. I don't want my parents to know it was me. They are worried enough."

"You have nothing to worry about. The New York Times contacted us too. They received the same set of documents that you delivered to the police. We have a gag order on the press that no names are to be released. All they can say is that the source was internal. We can't stop them from reporting the source. But they know we mean business and will keep your name out of the news."

"If there is a gag order, how has my name been connected to this case? I've been getting phone calls asking about my involvement with Sterling Chemicals about this case."

"They probably figured it out the same way that you did. But they are under the gag order as well. They cannot print anything or discuss anything involving your name."

"What about freedom of the press?"

"Well, there is 'freedom of the press' and 'freedom of the press' as it applies here."

"But..." Alex started.

"It makes our case stronger when we hear directly from you, and the interpretation of your findings. The documents only support your testimony. Regarding your phone calls, just say 'no comments'. Reporters then know that they will never get anything from you and will quit calling."

"But....." Alex started, but was cut off.

"You don't have to worry Dr. Gregory. We are here to support you. Let's get together so we can discuss this face to face."

"Won't it just be my word against their word?" Alex asked reciting what he heard on the TV cop shows. "And since I just started working for the company, there goes my credibility."

"That might be a problem, but we have other witnesses to support your findings and all the company's documents. We have also been doing an investigation ourselves. I can't discuss our findings with you at this time."

"If you have others, then you don't need me." Maybe some other employees must have come forth once the story broke; employees who have been with the corporation longer than he had. Alex was hoping with these new witnesses they would not need him.

"That is not exactly true. I believe you know the other two: Cindy Hudson and Leslie Sherwood. It didn't take us long to identify them once we found you Dr. Gregory. So, when are you available this week to come by and chat?"

Chat? That is strange way to express it Alex thought. This won't be a tea party.

"Do you really need to talk to them, too? You have me and you have the documents. They have been through so much already. I don't want to put them through more stress."

"We need to talk to them as well. They are needed to corroborate your testimony and they might remember something you don't. And, at this point, we are the only ones who know their names, so they have nothing to fear. And there is also a gag order on them too if anyone connects them to this case."

Alex stopped talking, trying to take all of this in and put his thoughts together before continuing. He was trying to think.

"Dr. Gregory?"

"Can the three of us meet with you at the same time then? I want to make sure that Leslie and Cindy are okay with this. And if I am there,

I know they will feel safe. We have been followed and stalked and have been in fear of our lives during the past month. I still have trouble sleeping at night and am always looking over my shoulder. They are probably going through the same. As I said, I want to make sure that they feel safe and I know they will be more comfortable if I am there with them."

"Don't worry Dr. Gregory, nothing will happen to them. All the people involved in this conspiracy are in custody."

"That is some comfort, but we are still on edge. What if there are others we don't know about? We have been followed, seen one of our colleagues run over and had to go into hiding for the past several weeks. We had just started the job and not even sure we have a job to go back to tomorrow. We are going back to Sterling tomorrow for the first time since this all started, hoping we still have a place with the company."

"I understand your concern Dr. Gregory. But you have done a great service in exposing a company that was about to release a product to the market, a product that had the potential to destroy life as we know it. Just realize what a great thing you have done for future generations."

"This experience is not something you shake off easily, if ever" Alex responded. "I would just feel better if I could be there when you meet with Cindy and Leslie."

"Of course, you can all meet with me as a group. But if they agree to meet one on one after the four of us meet, would you be okay with that?"

"If they agree and are not pressured into agreeing, I will be okay with it."

"Thank you for understanding."

"But if I feel they are being stressed when we meet the first time, the three of us will leave."

"I can live with that, and I will do everything I can to make them feel comfortable and safe."

There was a pause

"What is a good time for you? My schedule is open this week. I'd like to meet as soon as possible so we have plenty of time to prepare for the trial."

"Let me contact Leslie and Cindy and I'll get right back to you. I will have an answer for you sometime today."

"Thank you, Dr. Gregory. I'll be expecting your call. Again, don't worry. Let's get justice for the three people who lost their lives."

The phone went dead.

Three lives were gone...all in the name of greed Alex thought to himself.

Dawn, who worked for a senior vice president, was the first to disappear. She had discovered some discrepancies in accounting with a bank in Miami. She reported it to her boss, and shortly after that disappeared.

Then there was Peter, the person who had the job at Sterling before Alex. His death of a heart attack while on a business trip was ruled due to natural causes. A health issue that his wife Cindy, didn't believe was true. A meeting with Cindy and a hidden note taped to the back of a drawer in his desk, the desk assigned to Alex, started Alex on his quest for the truth.

And Brianna, an assistant to a senior vice president with a sense of loyalty to the company, provided Alex with confidential documents. As a result of removing the documents from the office, Brianna became the third victim of the cover-up.

The information provided by Brianna in conjunction with other information that Alex had uncovered, led him to the conclusion that members of senior manager were responsible for the deaths of Dawn, Peter, and Brianna.

Alex had turned the documents, along his suspicions, over to the police before he became the fourth victim. Then he, Leslie and Cindy went into hiding. Now out of hiding, he was being called to testify at their trial...testifying against senior management of a company that he had just joined. What had he gotten himself into?

Chapter 4

*A*lex heard a weird sound coming from the phone. He was sitting there with the phone in his hand long after Lisa Fisher had hung up. It was the phone screaming at him to 'hang up'. *Testimony? Why do they want my testimony? They have everything.* Pictures of TV court scenes rushed through his head. Images of a prosecuting attorney tearing the witness's testimony apart and exposing his personal life to the world went through his mind. *Is that how it really happens in a courtroom?*

Alex called Leslie. She answered after the first ring, as if she was expecting his call.

"Did you make the call Alex? Who are they...what did they want?"

"Yes, I made the call. It was from a Lisa Fisher from the District Attorney's office."

Alex heard a small gasp over the phone. He continued.

"They want to talk to us about the Sterling trial. They need to hear from us directly about our suspicions and findings. Even though they have all the documents we left with the police, they still want to talk to us."

"How did they find us Alex? Our names were never mentioned."

"That's my fault. I wasn't thinking. They traced us back through the courier company that delivered the documents to the police. Our names haven't been mentioned by the press yet because there is a gag order not to release that information. All the news can report is that the information came from an employee at Sterling."

"That is somewhat reassuring for now" she replied.

"The District Attorney wants to meet with us to get our story and also prepare us for our testimony in court" Alex added, prepared for a response from Leslie. It came back immediate with a loud high-pitched voice.

"Testimony?"

"Yes. They need us to testify in court. That is what the summons was all about. They want to talk to all of us to get our view on what we think happened. They also want to prepare us for our testimony."

"I've never talked to a lawyer in my life and now being called by the District Attorney. I thought this was all behind us."

Alex could hear fear in Leslie's voice.

"We will be okay Leslie. Remember, the bad guys are locked up. Also, I got the District Attorney to agree to meet with all three of us at the same time."

"So, Cindy got a notice too?"

"Yes, I called her right after I talked to you and told her I'd get back to her when I had more information. I told her not to do anything until she heard from me."

"I'm sure she is anxious right now. She has been through so much, with her husband being one of the victims and then having to go into hiding like we did."

"It was so nice of your parents to put her up until she was able to go to her sisters."

"My parents were perfectly happy to have both of you there. They would do anything to help us, especially when they realize what we have been through."

"I also enjoyed meeting them. Only wish it had been under different circumstances. Your dad was also a big asset in helping us find out who was behind a lot of this. He is also very proud of you Leslie for stepping forward like this."

"I'm glad you felt it was okay for him to know the whole story."

"We had to tell him or what would he think if all of a sudden I moved in for no particular reason."

"He would have thought we were shacking up together" Leslie added.

"Mmmmm... that sounds interesting."

"You are so bad" Leslie said with a lift in her voice.

"And you are too sweet" Alex responded.

"So, when do you think we should meet with the district attorney?" Leslie blurted out, louder than necessary.

"Here is what I think we should do. Let's go into work tomorrow as planned and see where we stand. We should know soon after we arrive. We either have a job or don't. The trial starts in a few weeks, I guess. So, I think we should meet with the DA as soon as possible. How about two o'clock tomorrow afternoon? Go into work and see if you still have a job. Then go downtown after lunch and get it over with."

"You are right. We need to do this so we can get on with our lives, whatever that may be. I just wish it was all behind us."

"I agree with you. I told the DA I'll get back to her this afternoon. Let me call Cindy and see if that works for her. Then I'll call the DA. So, we are set to meet tomorrow morning to go into work together and then downtown in the afternoon."

"Sounds like a plan."

Silence on the phone.

"Are you okay Leslie?" Alex asked.

"I'm fine, just trying to process everything that has happened. Thanks Alex…for everything."

"Bye Leslie. I miss not being with you."

"Bye Alex. Don't worry, I'm not going anywhere. I miss you too." The phone went dead.

Alex immediately dialed Cindy's number. Like Leslie, she picked up the phone after one ring. "Hi Cindy, Alex here. How are you doing?"

"Hi Alex. My phone started ringing right after we talked this morning and hasn't stopped. Reporters are trying to get an interview with me. Somehow, they found out that I was married to Peter and they want to know how I feel about Sterling and their part in Peter's death. I immediate hang up and am only answering calls from people I know. I'm trying to relax but not having much luck."

"Same thing has been happening here. I've unplugged my answering machine. It was full of message from people wanting to talk to me about the case. They haven't found Leslie yet. Our names were never published which is good. However, they found my name by tracking down the courier I used to deliver the package to the police. That was a stupid mistake on my part. I should have just dropped it off on the front steps and then run. The DA told me they have a gag order against publishing our names for now."

"That's the problem these days. We are all too connected" she replied. "It can be both good and bad."

There was a slight pause and then a loud voice "The DA. You talked to the District Attorney?"

"Yes, the number that we were all given was the office of the District Attorney. I called to see what they wanted. I talked to an attorney in the office, probably an Assistant DA…a Lisa Fisher. She wants to meet with the three of us to discuss the case. I convinced her to talk to all of us at the same time, rather than individually. I told her I would call back this afternoon and set up a meeting after I had talked to you and Leslie. The trial starts in a few weeks, so we need to do this as soon as possible."

"When do you have in mind?"

"I suggested to Leslie that we meet tomorrow afternoon about two o'clock. We both want to go into the office in the morning and see if we still have jobs."

"You're right let's get it over with. How about I meet you in front of your office at two o'clock tomorrow afternoon and we will all go downtown together? Since Peter worked there for years, I know where the building is located."

"That sounds good. Are you doing okay?"

"I'm doing fine. It is good to be home and I want to put all of this behind me. How is Leslie doing?"

"She's trying to be strong, but I know inside she is scared. I think we all are at some level. After all, we have been spied upon, followed and witnessed the death of Brianna. We have a right to be scared and anxious."

There was silence on the phone, and then Cindy spoke softly.

"Alex, you have carried most of the burden this past month. Without you to watch over us, I don't know what Leslie and I would have done. How are you doing?"

"I'm fine. Thanks Cindy. You two have been great and we make a good team. We are strong for each other."

"You have been our strength. Thanks for everything Alex. Without you I wouldn't have known the truth about Peter. Bye Alex." With that Cindy hung up leaving him standing there with the phone in his hand.

Hanging up he looked out the window at the Hudson River. Across the river he could see New Jersey. Everything looked so calm and peaceful, not a ripple on the surface of the water and a barge slowly moving up the river toward the George Washington Bridge. He wished his life was as calm as the river.

Picking up the piece of paper he had left on the table next to the sofa, he dialed the number of the District Attorney's office to set up the time for the meeting tomorrow.

Chapter 5

Alex was standing in front of the Sterling Chemicals building at 8:20 am. Having been away for a month, it was as if he were seeing it for the first time. He purposely arrived before Leslie so she wouldn't be anxious waiting for him too arrived. Dressed in business casual he fit in with all the other people entering the building.

As he stood there, he wondered what would happen once he entered the sixty-two-floor skyscraper in front of him. He left the building one day about a month ago and never came back. He wondered what rumors about his disappearance circulated through the department. Also, did he even have a job? What lies ahead once he enters the building? What did his colleagues believed happened to him?

First, if they believed he were dead, he wouldn't be able to get pass the lobby. TV News Stations had reported that a car he had rented had gone off the road in New Jersey into the Hudson River. No bodies were found but that is not unusual due to the currents in the river. But without a body there was no poof he was dead. Maybe the company concluded that he just got up and left the job for an unknown reason. It was not their responsibility to determine where he was. Either way, his badge would have been deactivated.

Secondly, if his badge is still activated, he might get to his office and find it empty and then be escorted out of the building. Or he might arrive at his office and find someone else sitting at his desk.

Thirdly he would find his office as he had left it and he would settle in and start the day as if nothing ever happened. Whatever the outcome, he had no idea how he would react. He would just have to wait and see.

Just then Leslie emerged from the subway entrance that opened in front of the building, looking as beautiful as when he saw her for the first time. He would rather look at her than at the glass and steel building in front of him. She was even wearing the same dark-blue outfit she wore the day he first laid eyes on her. Her deep mahogany hair hung to her shoulders bouncing as she walked toward him. Her features were flawless… smooth skin and the perfect nose any model would envy. She gave him a slight wave as she approached. When she reached him, she displayed that perfect smile. As usual, he felt excitement at seeing her.

"Good morning, Alex. Well, here we are, back where we started" she said as she looked up at the talk building.

"It is so good to see you, looking as beautiful as ever." He wanted to take her in his arms and kiss her deeply.

"You always say the nicest things" she replied with that effervescent smile.

"The big moment…do we still work here? Or are we out on the street? If they believe the news that we are somewhere in the Hudson River we won't get past security because our badges would have been deactivated. Time to go find out if we are alive or dead" Alex added, trying to lighten the moment.

Leslie stared at the front door and then back at Alex. Her face showed concern. Alex grabbed her hand.

"Ready to go" he asked?

"I've wanted this day to come since we left the city a month ago. But now, I'm not so sure" she replied, looking up at the skyscraper before her. "Up there on the sixty-first floor is where it all started" she added, still looking upward. There is an empty desk up there that once belonged to me for a short period of time.

"We can't put it off any longer. We knew eventually we would have to come back, even if only to get our personal items. Let's march in as if we belong here."

They joined the other employees entering the building after a weekend of rest. Taking out their employee badge, they headed to the turnstile for employees. They both slowed their pace, concerned about this first test…are we alive or dead?

They swiped their employee badge across the card reader. The light turned green and they went through.

"Well we passed the first test and we are alive" Alex said softly to Leslie.

"Or no one told security" Leslie added.

"Now let's see if we make it upstairs. Do you want me to come up with you?"

"Thanks Alex, but I need to do this alone and you need to get to your floor and see what happens.

"Promise to call me as soon as you know something" Alex said looking at Leslie, forcing a smile of confidence. "I'll wait for your call."

"I'll call or text you as soon as I can…and you let me know your status as well. Promise?"

"I promise." Again, he wanted to take her in his arms.

Alex walked with Leslie to a single elevator separated from the rest of the elevators, an elevator only for the executives on the top two floors. Since Leslie worked for an executive VP, she had access to that elevator. She swiped he employee badge over the card reader. The elevator door opened, she stepped in and inserted her badge into the card reader. As the door closed, she softly said 'good luck'. But he also saw concern in her eyes. He wished he had kissed her for good luck, but knew it was not the time or place. He stood and watched the numbers on the display panel over the door. The elevator stopped on the sixty-first floor. Leslie made it to her floor with no problem. Now, his turn.

Alex moved back to the bank of elevators for 'regular' employees. The employees gathered in the hallway of the elevator banks, waiting for the next elevator door to open. No one paid any attention to him.

That is a good sign he thought to himself. He heard a woman make mention of the upcoming trial. Another person was talking about the effect on the company this scandal would have and if there would be layoffs because of the huge drop in the Company's stock price. Alex just stood there, watching the numbers on the panel over the doors as the elevator descended. Behind him someone said, "I think I better start looking for a new job."

Just then the elevator arrived on the first floor, the doors opened, and everyone pushing their way in.

Alex waited for everyone else to push the button for their floor. No one pushed forty-two. He reached around a guy and pushed the button. Again, no one paid any attention to him. The doors of the elevator closed, and they were on their way up.

Alex felt sweat start to form on his forehead from anticipation of what was in store for him when he reached his floor. He didn't want to wipe it off so as not to bring attention to it. He only hoped no one noticed.

The elevator stopped and the doors opened on the forty-second floor and he stepped out. He was the only one to get off the elevator. The doors closed behind him and he was alone in the hallway. In front of him he saw rows of cubes in front of offices that lined both walls. Offices for the regulars; cubes for support staff.

Here I go he thought.

◆

The door of the private elevator opened on the sixty-first floor and Leslie stepped out. Back to where she started. She just stood there looking around, not sure what to expect.

In front of her were three large cubes, set aside for the assistant assigned to each of the Vice Presidents. One cube was hers. Three large offices and private conference rooms opened into the center area, one for each of the three vice presidents who occupied this floor. There was also a file room, three conference rooms and a kitchen that made up the remainder of this area. The mahogany wood floor was covered with a plush carpet. In the distance was a glass wall with a door in the middle that separated this executive area from the hallway with a bank of elevators for visitors to use.

On the other side of the glass wall was a reception area, composed of a mahogany desk for the receptionist. Behind the desk was a sitting area it with 4 large leather chairs and two leather sofas. Each chair had a mahogany table next to it with a crystal lamp and telephone. A large rug covered the floor under the chairs. The elevators doors were on the wall opposite the reception desk.

There was no one sitting at the desk, usually occupied by Barb, the first-person Leslie met when she started working. *Where is Barb?* Leslie thought. *I hope she is still with the company.*

Everything was quiet, not a person in sight. Six weeks ago, this floor was buzzing with activity. The two other assistants, Brianna and Rob, would be in their cubes working away on their computer or on the phone. The three Vice Presidents would be on the phone talking to people all over the world …now nothing.

Leslie heard a noise and looked toward the coffee room. Barb came through the door carrying a cup of coffee. She looked up and saw Leslie standing there, as if she were seeing a ghost. Barb hesitated for a few seconds, put the coffee cup down on a file cabinet and rushed toward Leslie.

Leslie took a step back, not knowing what to expect. Barb rushed over and put her arms around her. She held the hug longer than usual. Leslie just stood there stiff as a board. Slowly she put her arms around Barbara. A few seconds later Barbara pulled away and grabbed Leslie's hands.

"I have been so worried about you Leslie. I heard on the news that you had been in an automobile accident and the car went over the edge of the Palisades into the Hudson River. A week went by and no word of you. I was sure we had lost you but hoped I was wrong. Then one day Mr. Sterling came down and told me in confidence that you were okay, but I had to keep it a secret. I cried happy tears for about an hour. I'm so glad that you are here and are okay" putting her arms around Leslie again giving her a big hug, refusing to let go.

"Thanks Barb. I wasn't sure if I would even be welcomed back. I'm still not sure."

"Leslie, how silly of you" Barb said, releasing Leslie and looking at her through tearful eyes. Of course. you are welcomed back. I've missed you. It has been rather boring here all alone. Come, let's get you settled at your desk and then we can catch up."

So, I still have a desk Leslie thought. A sign of relief came from deep within her.

"But first let's make sure your badge still works to get into this area. If not, I will take care of it."

Barb turned and headed toward the glass wall, with Leslie following. The glass door automatically opened as they approached. They stepped through and they heard the door click as it locked behind them.

"Okay, let's see if your badge still works on the card reader. The new security code is 6575."

Leslie swiped her card over the card reader to the right of the door and punched in the four-digit code on the keypad. She heard a click and the door opened automatically. Her cards still worked. She let out a sign of relief…she was still employed.

They entered the inner sanctum. Just then the phone at the reception desk started to ring.

"Mr. Sterling wants to meet you Leslie. I have instructions to call him as soon as you show up."

"Can you wait and call him a little later? I need to get settled first and make a phone call."

"I understand but I can't wait long. His secretary has been calling to see if I have heard from you. I'm also sure that they have been notified that you are here once you swiped your badge when you entered the building on the first floor. They probably also saw you on the cameras in the private elevator."

"Just give me a few minutes. I just need to calm down. It won't be long."

"Okay. I need to go back out front. The phones have been ringing non-stop. Just let me know when you are ready so I can call Mr. Sterling and tell him you are here. I'm so glad that you are back. I've worried about you."

"Thanks Barb, but there was no need to worry, I was in good hands."

Barb gave Leslie another hug and simply said "Welcome back." Leslie watched as Barb returned to her area on the other side of the glass wall.

Leslie turned and looked around. It was so quiet here. When she started the company a month ago there were seven people on this floor. Phones would be ringing, people talking, visitors coming and going. Now there was only Barb that she could see. Now it was dead quiet.

As she headed to her work area, she saw Brianna's station in front of her. She stood and looked at it, tears forming in her eyes. Brianna Welch, the queen bee of the sixty-first floor.

Brianna appeared to be distant and put on an air of authority with no friends at Sterling when Leslie first met her. But she turned out to be a very caring person. Her concern for Leslie's and Alex's safety led to her death and probably saved theirs. With tears still in her eyes, she moved past Brianna work area, slowly running her fingers over her desk as she did.

Leslie then looked to Rob's cubicle. No tears for him. Rob Schimel, the All-American-Boy currently charged with Brianna's death and now sitting in a jail cell at Riker's Island.

The third cubicle was hers. It was exactly as she left it. She looked at the three VP offices along the outer wall, with floor to ceiling windows looking across the Manhattan skyline.

Leslie looked toward the first office. The door was closed. and the lights were off. This was the office of Mr. Alan Milton, Sr. VP of

Operations and R&D. According to the news, he resigned from the company after the news of the cover-up was made public.

She looked at the next office, also with the door closed and lights off. It was the office of Mr. Tony Gianti, Sr. VP of Finance and IT. No tears here. Like Rob, he was at Riker's Island, locked in a cell waiting for his trial. He was charged for being the master mind behind all the murders that took place to protect the company's secrets and his big paycheck.

The last office belonged to Mr. Curtis Clark, Sr. VP of Production and Manufacturing, and Leslie's boss. The door was open and the lights on and papers all over the desk. But there was no one in the office. According to the news, he had also resigned from the company.

Resigned or forced out? Leslie thought.

As Leslie moved to her desk, she wondered who was occupying that office. She sat at her desk wondering what to do next. There was nothing for her to do. She turned on her computer out of habit. Her password worked so she is still in the system. She opened her purse to take out her cell phone to text Alex to let him know that everything was okay. She heard the private elevator door open and close. She couldn't see the elevator from here desk so listened for footsteps but heard nothing. She went back to her cell phone and started to text Alex when she felt someone behind her. Stopping what she was doing, she swirled her chair around to see if anyone was there. Stand there looking at her was a tall man in a business suit.

"Good Morning Ms. Sherwood. I'm Charles Sterling, CEO of the company. We have never officially been introduced."

Chapter 6

*A*s Alex walked to his office on the forty-second floor, no one looked at him in a strange way. Everyone just went about their business.

They probably don't recognize me since I am so new to the company and hadn't really been here all that much, he thought to himself.

Sitting right outside his office was his assistant, Lindsey at her workstation, her back to him.

"Good morning Lindsey."

Lindsey turned in her chair and there was a look of surprise on her face.

"Dr. Gregory!" is all she could say.

"Good to see you too" he said as he turned and went into his office. Everything was as he had left it, just like his apartment. At least no one had moved in while he was gone. He moved around his desk and sat in his chair not knowing what to do next.

The same old lumps in the chair he thought with a smile on his face. His eyes then focused on the desk drawer to his right. It was there that he found the note hidden by Peter; the note that started the search to find the truth about the new product, 57162 and what it meant to the company and upper management…and how dangerous it was to the environment.

Lindsey appeared in the doorway. "You're back" is all she could stay, with surprise in her voice.

"Did you think I wouldn't return? Come in and shut the door."

Alex watched as she shut the door and quickly moved to the chair across the desk, never taking her eyes off him.

Lindsey Meyer looked exactly as she did when Alex saw her a month ago. Her short brown hair just covering her ears, parted in the middle, every strand in place. It was hard to miss her green eyes as she looked at you. Her mouth had a slight dip on the right side which gave her face character. It wasn't noticeable unless you looked for it, but it added a mystery to her. Her makeup was flawless, and her clothes looked as if they were made for her. Alex guessed her age to be in her late twenties. In fact, he knew very little about her life outside of the office. He assumed she was single since he didn't see a wedding ring on her finger.

"You looked surprised to see me" Alex stated.

"I didn't think I would ever see you again. No idea why I thought that, but it was the only scenario that keep going through my head… especially after the reports on TV."

"Well, here I am. Can you bring me up to date what is happening around here?" Alex asked, choosing his words carefully.

"You don't know?"

"I'm not sure what I know, so why not tell me."

"First of all, we all saw the television news where they reported you might have drowned in the Hudson River. Everyone was upset. It was the talk of the office. But when no body was found, we started to doubt the news. But as the days went by rumors started that you had been washed out to sea and we would never see you again…everyone was convinced you were dead. The Hudson River is not forgiving. Even then it was hard to comprehend. You had just started working here. Many of the people in the department had never met you but just knew your name. All kinds of rumors circulated of how it happened."

"What kind of rumors?"

"First of all, people started to think that this office was bad luck. You were the second person to occupy it who died unexpectedly. Did you know that Peter Hudson died of a heart attack while on a business trip? No one understood how he could have had a heart attack since he was in such good physical shape. But it happened."

"I knew of Peter's death and the circumstances around it. Mr. Mathews told me about him the first day I was here" Alex lied. He had learned the details of Peter's death from Cindy, Peter's wife, who had helped him uncovered the real cause of her husband's death.

"I worked for him too. People jokingly said I must be jinxed."

"I'm sure you aren't jinxed. What other kind of things were people saying when they heard of my 'reported' death?

"The first thing was that maybe you had been drinking and went over the cliff. From there other rumors and ideas started to circulate around the office."

"Like what?" Alex asked.

"Some suspected that maybe you were on your cell phone; or a deer ran in front of you; or someone sideswiped you. No matter what they said, you were still dead. And later it was learned that there might have been other people in the car with you. And then the rumors started that the other people in the car with you also worked here. But no bodies had been found.

Alex saw no need to confirm or deny the rumors.

"Then the gossip was that the other person in the car worked for some executive here and that the two of you were involved in the police business here."

"What police business?" Alex asked, trying to appear surprised.

"About a week after your disappearance, all hell broke loose here. We heard that the police entered the building and took several people away in handcuffs. Later we learned that it was one of the VP's and his assistant as well as a consultant. They were all arrested for murder. It has been all over the news."

"Murder?" Alex exclaimed. Who was murdered?

"The only name that people have been passing around was Dawn Manning from the finance department. I didn't know her. Some people also speculated Peter had been murdered and that they might have being responsible for your disappearance. Some even thought that you might have been the employee who blew the whistle on the company and as a result you were a victim. Of course, I didn't believe that. I knew you were okay and would be back"

"As you can see, I'm here and I'm okay just as you thought. Why would anyone think I had anything to do with blowing the whistle on the company as you put it? I've only been here a short time. I hardly know my way around this floor."

"That is what I told everyone who suggested that. We also heard that several other VP's were fired soon after the arrests. Haven't you been watching TV? And by the way, where exactly have you been?"

"I've been away on a business trip" is all Alex could think of saying. He knew Lindsey wouldn't buy that for a second. But he also knew she wouldn't question it.

Alex quickly changed the conversation. "Yes, I saw the TV reports. But since I didn't know any of the people involved, I kind of ignored it. Since I was away, I'm just interested in getting your perspective of what has been going in the office. You were here while all of this has happened."

Apparently, his name has not been seriously linked to the police business. Nor has Leslie's or Cindy's. The police gag order worked.

"I was so upset that I wasn't able to concentrate on my work" Lindsey continued. And every day I had to come in here and look at your empty office not knowing where you were, just like I had to do after Peter's death. Apparently, Mr. Matthews noticed how upset I was, or someone told him I was taking your disappearance very hard. One day out of the blue he called me into his office. He has never called me into his office. He was very comforting though. He made me feel better. I sensed however that he wanted to tell me something but didn't. He just kept saying, 'everything will be okay, just hang in there'"

"Why did you think he was hiding something?"

"It just seemed that he was choosing his words very carefully. I just felt he knew more than he was saying. Then when I left his office, I started thinking what he said. I decided in my mind that he knew what happened to you but couldn't tell me. He was just trying to soften the blow when I finally found out the truth."

"What did you think he wasn't telling you?"

"That you had died in that accident" she replied, looking straight at Alex.

"Apparently people started to believe that too" she continued "since you had been gone so long and no one has heard anything. Soon the rumors stopped, and people quit asking me about you. As the days went on, I started to believe that too, even though I didn't want it to be true. Everyone had turned their attention to what will happy to the company and their jobs. That is why I was so surprised when you walked in this morning. I thought you were dead and someplace in the Atlantic Ocean as fish food."

"I guess you were wrong" Alex said with smile.

"I sure was. I totally misread what Mr. Mathews meant. I guess it is human nature to go to the dark side when all the evidence points that way."

"I'm sorry you had to go through that. But as you can see, I'm back and I'm not fish food."

"So, where have you been?" Leslie asked again, staring intently at Alex's face, and still sitting on the edge of the chair.

"I was away on company business. It had to be kept a secret. Mr. Mathews knew about it. He is the one who sent me" Alex lied.

"I guess I read him wrong. He was trying to tell me that you were okay."

"The important thing is that I am back, and everything is okay." Alex stated. knowing that Lindsey wouldn't be satisfied with that answer. But he also knew that she wouldn't pressure for more information.

There was a knock on Alex's door. They both turned to see Jeanette Braun standing in the doorway. "Welcome back Dr. Gregory."

"Hello Jeanette. Thank you." Alex replied.

"Mr. Mathews would like to see you right now Dr. Gregory." Don Mathews was Alex's boss and Jeanette was his assistant. This interruption gave Alex a chance to leave his office and not have to answer any more of Lindsey's questions.

Alex got up and followed Jeanette down the hall. "Good to see you Jeanette" he said as they walked down the hallway toward his boss's office.

"Good to have you back" was all she said. She had always been very business-like. Here is another co-worker that Alex knew very little about.

As Jeanette walked just slightly in front of him, he noticed her wide hips swing gracefully with each step. Her back was perfectly straight, and her head rose as if saying 'look at me and how important I am.' Her hair was a mixture of brown and gray and she wore it in a bun on the back of her head. Eyeglasses hung on a chain bouncing against her ample breasts with each step she took. If he had to describe her dress, he would say vintage but stylish; made for comfort rather than show but worn with class.

Alex checked his cell phone as they walked to his boss's office. No message from Leslie.

When they arrived at Mr. Mathews' office Jeanette stepped aside and let Alex enter. She then shut the door leaving him alone in the office.

Mr. Mathews got up from his chair and motioned to an area in his office with two sofas facing each other, a mahogany coffee table between them. "Let's sit over there" he said.

Alex sat on the sofa opposite Mr. Mathew, waiting for him to lead the conversation.

"First of all, welcome back Alex."

"Thank you, sir" was all Alex said.

"So how are you doing?"

"I'm doing fine. Thank you for asking. Of course, I am wondering whether or not I still have a job?"

"Of course. you still have a job here" he said with a light laugh in his voice.

Alex just got his confirmation that he was still employed.

"I've sorry I had to be away so long without letting anyone know where I was."

"At first we were concerned. We had no idea what happened. Then all this police activity started, and your absence was put on the back burner so to say."

"Police Activity?" Alex asked, not knowing if Gene knew his part in the whole thing.

"I'm sure you know that the company has been going through some major changes. You are too smart of a guy not to know what has been going on. You remember, I hired you and know you well."

"And I'm glad you did hire me. It is a great opportunity to work for a company concerned with the environment and helping people with better food products" Alex responded trying to get the subject away from his absence.

"Mr. Sterling has asked me to help him rebuild the marketing department and company strategies. I have been spending most of my time on the executive floor. I suspect there will be a lot of changes in the direction of this company."

Just then the phone rang. Gene walked to his desk to answer it. "Yes sir, he is here now." There was a pause as Gene listened to the person on the other end of the phone. Apparently, they were taking about him. "Yes sir, I'll send him right up."

Gene hung up the phone and turned to Alex.

"Mr. Sterling would like to see you right now."

"The CEO wants to see me?" is all Alex could respond.

"Yes, he is waiting in his office on the 62nd floor. You better be on your way."

"Why does he want to see me?" Alex asked as Gene walked with him to the elevator.

Gene said nothing as they walked the rest of the way to the elevator. Alex watched the numbers change above the door; the elevator coming up from the first floor. The door opened and Alex entered. Gene reached in and pushed the elevator button for the top floor. As the door closed, he looked at Alex, smiled and said softly "I know all about you and where you have been."

Chapter 7

*T*he elevator stopped on the 62nd floor, the door opened, and Alex stepped out. He was the only person on the elevator the entire trip. The doors closed and he stood alone on the top floor of the building. The walls at the end of the reception area to the left and right were glass, floor to ceiling, looking up and down Park Avenue. A plush oriental carpet covered the high-glossed wood floor. His feet sunk into the softness of the carpet. There was a small sitting area to the right and left of him. In front of him was a wall of teak wood with two black glass doors in the center that showed his reflection. To the right of the door was a large mahogany desk with a security guard. The entire floor was for the sole use of Charles Sterling, CEO of Sterling Chemicals. Beside his personal office it had the Company Board Room and various visitor's offices.

Sterling Chemicals started over one hundred years ago by two brothers in Ohio. Their first product was a high-pressure catalytic process to synthesize ammonia directly from nitrogen and hydrogen. The process was later used in the synthesis of methanol and hydrogenation of coal to petroleum. Early in the twentieth century, their work on long-chained molecules provided the foundation for plastics and synthetic fibers. Sterling Chemicals took advantage of these new technologies and expanded into other areas.

Although the company still produced raw materials for other industries, its focus was now on the development of products to increase the world's food supply. This included new compounds to control pests on plants and stored crops, new plant varieties, and ways to increase crop yield.

The corporate headquarters moved from Ohio to Manhattan in 1953 and to the current location on Park Avenue in 1958. The gross income of the company reached over a billion dollars last year. The company employed over forty-five thousand people in the United States and Canada and over eighty thousand worldwide. Alex was one of their newest.

Turning left he could see all the way uptown to the Bronx and then turn turning right he could see all the way downtown to Wall Street and the Statue of Liberty standing proudly in the harbor.

Taking a breath, he walked to desk.

"I'm here to See Mr. Sterling."

"May I have your name?"

"Alex Gregory."

"One moment please." The guard picked up the phone and talked to someone on the other end. Hanging up he turned back to Alex. "Through those doors" he said pointing to the doors behind him. Someone will meet you on the other side." Short and to the point, not even a hello or a smile.

Alex walked toward the glass doors. They didn't look like doors, but two large mirrors in the center of wooden wall that separated this reception area from the rest of the floor. As he got close to the doors, he heard a click and the doors silently slide open.

A woman was waiting for him on the other side of the doors. Her arms were folded as if waiting was a waste of her time. Her face had no expression. She was dressed in a gray tailored business suit. Her hair was arranged in a matronly style. Her gray eyes seemed to pierce right through you. Not a visible wrinkle on her face but there were streaks of gray in her coal black hair. A pair of glasses sat on the top of her head. Alex could not guess her age.

"Welcome Dr. Gregory. I'm Kathryn Meyer, Mr. Sterling's private secretary. Mr. Sterling is waiting for you. Follow me please."

She turned and headed toward the back wall of this large open area. Alex followed in step behind her. As they walked to the back of the floor, Alex turned and noticed that the door he came through was a one-way mirror. He was able to see out into the reception area.

They passed a large room on the left. The door was open, and Alex could see a large table in the center and large leather back chairs around it. The end wall of that room was floor to ceiling windows looking out over Manhattan. Opposite the conference room, on the other side of the open area, were individual offices that appeared to be undergoing renovation. The back of each office was a wall of windows looking downtown, each having a view of the Statue of Liberty. In front of each office was a workstation, none of which showed any sign of being occupied.

At the end of the large space was the office of the CEO of Sterling Chemicals, Charles Sterling. The entire wall was glass looking into his office. Through it, Alex could see a large desk at one end. On a credenza to the right of the desk were two monitors, one constantly changing showing changes in the stock market.

At the other end of the office was a fireplace against a wooden wall. In front of the fireplace were two leather sofas. A very distinguished man with gray hair was sitting on one of the sofas. Alex assumed that was Mr. Sterling. Across from him was a woman with her back to Alex. As they approached the door to the office the man stood up and the woman looked over her shoulder. It was Leslie and when she saw Alex, a big smile came over her face.

Mr. Sterling met Alex at the office door. "Welcome Dr. Gregory. Come join us. I'm Charles Sterling" he said as he extended his hand. "And I believe you know Ms. Sherwood."

"Thank you, sir nice to meet you. Yes, I know Ms. Sherwood. Hi Leslie."

"Hi Alex."

Alex moved to the sofa where Leslie was sitting. He stood there not knowing what to do.

Charles Sterling, CEO of Sterling Chemicals, had inherited his position from his father who had inherited it from his father, the founder of the company. Alex was surprised how short he was. You expect the CEO of a company to be a large stately man. Alex guessed him to be about five foot eight inches tall. He must eat well and exercise because he appeared to be in good shape. He was wearing a custom made dark blue suit that fit the contours of his body like a glove. It was strange to see a suit since everyone else in the company seemed to be wearing "business casual". His hair was a dark brown with no signs of gray, but his face looked worn.

"Please, sit" Mr. Sterling said, pointing to the sofa where Leslie was sitting. Alex sat down next to Leslie and Charles Sterling sat in the sofa opposite the two.

"First of all, welcome back to work."

"Thank you, sir. It is good to be back." Alex waited to see what would happen next.

"I want to assure both of you that you still have a position here at Sterling, and I feel honored that I have two such loyal employees working for this company."

Alex could feel a sign of relief escape from his chest and sure Leslie felt the same.

"I have spent many hours with the police and am very upset that I inadvertently put you two at risk. I hope you will accept my apology. I am making changes to assure that nothing like this ever happens again. I understand Alex, that you were the prime instigator into the investigation of this new product and how dangerous it was."

"Sir, all three of us were involved in the discovery. I would have to say that Cindy Hudson was the catalyst in getting this going. She lost her husband because of this product."

"Yes, Cindy Hudson. I have already talked to her and thanked her for your work and provided my condolence for the loss of her husband. I have authorized her husband's salary to be given to her for the next five years. That includes all bonuses and I will pay all taxes. It is the least I can do for her loss. I have also offered her a position with Sterling. Not surprising however, she said she wanted to discuss her options with you two first."

"That is very generous of you sir."

"I've also done the same for Dawn Manning and Brianna Welch's family.

"Thank you, sir. I didn't know Dawn, but Brianna took a big risk for this company. She loved it here and was a loyal employee."

"I only wish that I were more aware of what my executives were doing. That has all changed. I'm going to be more hands on and in touch with the day to day activities around the company."

Silence…

"As you can see, there is remodeling happening on this floor. I'm going to move my Sr. Vice Presidents to this floor so I can keep a pulse on what is happening in the company. That means that you will be moving up to this to this floor too Leslie. I am also promoting you to a senior position and you will have responsibility for training and overseeing the other assistants. You will be reporting to Ms. Meyer's."

"Thank you, sir" is all Leslie could say.

"And Barb will move up also and be promoted to an assistant position."

"Congratulations Leslie" Alex said looking at her and giving a big smile.

"I have to rebuild my senior staff with people who care about our customers and the company mission. I've already filled one position. Your boss, Gene Mathews will be moving up here and will handle the company's marketing and new product efforts. We have already begun the search for his replacement."

"I'm sure he will do a good job sir."

"…and as a start" he continued "I want you two to help be the eyes and ears around the company. You will always have access to me, and you will have my private phone number. If you accept this role there are only two conditions that I ask of you."

Both Alex and Leslie looked at each other and then turned back to Charles Sterling so as not to miss a single word.

"First, only the three of us and my private secretary must ever know you have been given this authority, inside or outside the company. We don't know who knows who."

"Second, before contacting me about something that is bothering you, you will discuss it between yourselves and decide together whether I need to get involved. No issue is too large or too small to discuss, but only if you both agree it is important and needs my attention. At this point I trust your judgement. If Ms. Hudson joins the company, she will be added to the group after being here six months and you both agree that she be added."

"That is quite a responsibility to put on two new employees sir" Alex added. "I'm sure there are more seasoned personal that would be more fitting for that role."

"Yes, there are many people who have been here a long time and know how the company runs and how I think. That is a disadvantage to them. They would view everything the same way it has been done in the past. You two, bring an entire new and fresh look to the company. And more important you showed that you are willing to take the steps to do something about it…that is the key component you bring to the party."

"Thank you" Leslie added. "I hope we can live up to your expectations."

"I have total faith in my decision. I have had time to think about this for a while. Now let me also make it clear that I don't want you to go looking for things to report, but only address things that you run across that you don't feel fits the philosophy of the company and our mission."

"I understand sir. Thank you for your confidence in us" Alex replied.

"Of course, I will ask you to sign a confidentiality agreement. It will not be in your personal file for others to see. It will be filed up here. Ms. Meyer's will get the agreement to you in the next couple of days to review and sign."

"Thank you for your confidence in us" Alex repeated.

One other thing I forgot to mention. There will be a $10,000 appreciation figure in your next paycheck and a 3% increase in salary effective immediately."

"Thank you." They both said at the same time.

"But you have to pay the taxes" he said with a smile. You three have saved the company millions of dollars in potential lawsuits, as well as saving the reputation of the company. No dollar amount could be placed on that."

"Sir, Leslie and I have been summoned to meet with the District Attorney regarding this situation. We were planning on meeting this afternoon. I hope that is okay."

"Of course, take the rest of the day off. They probably want to hear your side of the story before the trial starts and prepare you for your testimony. Take whatever time you need until this is all settled. Keep any monetary receipt involved with this case so you can get reimbursed."

"Thank you."

With that Mr. Sterling stood up. It was a sign that the meeting was over. He escorted them to his office door.

"Thank you for your service to the company and to me. Keep up the good work" shaking their hands while looking sincerely into their eyes. "Ms. Meyer will show you out." With that, he turned and moved to his desk, picking up the phone as he sat down, leaving Leslie and Alex standing alone outside his office.

"I think this has been a good day so far" Alex remarked. "Not bad, a promotion after only two months. You must know someone" Alex added.

"I do...I know you."

Ms. Meyer moved over to them from her desk.

"Welcome to the team Leslie. It will be a pleasure to have you with us" she said with a slight smile. "Now if you follow me, I will take you to the elevator."

As they passed through the area, Leslie looked around taking in her new working environment. So much had happened since she started here two months ago.

"We will talk soon" Ms. Meyer said as the two moved into the outer hallway. As they passed through the doorway, Leslie turned and said. 'thank you' and watched her new boss move swiftly back into the inner area, the doors shutting behind her. So many thoughts were going through her head.

"Now let's get lunch and meet Cindy and see what other surprises lie ahead for us" Alex said while they waited for the elevator.

Alex was right, what surprises will they find next?

Chapter 8

*C*indy was waiting in front of the office building when Leslie and Alex exited.

"Have you been waiting long?" Alex asked.

"Less than five minutes; this is a good spot for people watching anyway. It is like watching a bunch of ants running around; everyone in a hurry, most of them on their cell phones. It always surprises me that more don't run into each other. However, one guy was so busy texting on his phone that he fell off the curb. He caught himself from totally falling to the ground. And no one around him paid any attention."

"It's the world we live in" Leslie said. "Everyone feels they must be connected at all times. It is like they need self-assurance that they exist."

"Are we all psyched up for what lies ahead?" Alex asked.

"I wish this was all behind us and we could get back to a normal life" Leslie added.

"I don't think there will be a normal life for us soon. What is a normal life for us anyway? We haven't had time to establish a daily pattern...at least I haven't. We are all starting a part of our life that is new to us...we've never been here before." Alex added, putting his arm around Leslie. "Maybe what lies ahead is normal for us. You will be okay, we all will. We've been through a lot worse. This is going to be like a walk in the park."

"Some walk" Leslie added, a smirk on her face. "More like a walk on a stormy day."

"Let's grab a cab and head downtown and see what the District Attorney wants. Someone remind me to get a receipt."

Alex stepped to the curb looking uptown for an empty cab heading in his direction. About three minutes passed before one came around the corner. Alex stepped off the curb and waved his arms to flag it down before anyone else got the cab's attention. The cab pulled over and Alex opened the back door. Cindy got in and slid across the back seat, followed by Leslie, who sat in the middle, and then Alex got in, closing the door behind him.

"Where to bud?" the drive asked.

Alex looked up at him and yelled through the plastic divider separating the front from the back seat. "Number One Hogan Place please."

The driver turned on the meter, put the car in gear and pulled away from the curb. He looked as if he hadn't shaved in a few days and his hair was all tousled. Probably because his window was open. His shirt was wrinkled and hung loosely over his chest. Alex noticed that both arms were covered with tattoos. He couldn't make out if there was a theme to the tattoos but guessed they ran all the way up his arm and covered his shoulders, too.

During the trip downtown, no one said anything. Alex turned to Leslie. She looked straight ahead; eyes fixed on the street as they headed downtown. Not an emotion on her face. Alex grabbed her hand. She turned to him.

"Alex…it just registered with me that Mr. Sterling said…we will have to testify in court. I have never been in a court room. All I can think of is how the witnesses are treated by the defense lawyers on television. Their lives are displayed for all to see. That scares me."

"That's television. I'm sure it is not like that in real life. We have done nothing wrong and have nothing to hide."

"I'm not sure that applies to me" Leslie said softly, as if talking to herself.

Alex felt it best not to address that statement at this time.

"They always bring up bad things that have happened in your past to discredit you. And we will have to face Tony and Rob, the two responsible for Peter's and Brianna's death."

After saying that Leslie remembered she was sitting next to Cindy, Peter's wife. She turned to see Cindy looking straight ahead with a sad look on her face. She was probably thinking about Peter.

"I'm sorry Cindy. I wasn't thinking" Leslie said taking her hand.

"That's okay. We are all concerned about the trial. Like you I'm kind of worried too. But then I think of Peter and how brave he was. I have to do this for him."

"We all have to," Alex stated "and for Brianna, too. The bad guys are all in jail and will stay there. Leslie, I'm sure you have nothing in your past that you need to worry about."

Alex glanced over at Leslie and noticed a strange look on her face. She was probably just anxious. That look on her face wouldn't go away in his mind. *Did she have something to hide?*

"All of a sudden this is becoming very real and we seem to be in the middle of it" Leslie added, continuing to look straight ahead. "And I have to face those guys again."

"We just have to stay strong as we have been and tell the truth. Let the police and District Attorney do the rest."

"I know I should feel that way, but my head is saying something else."

"Leslie, you have been so strong and brave through this ordeal" Cindy interjected. "I'm so proud of you and Alex, and I know that Peter is looking down on us and feels the same."

Silence…that look still on Leslie's face.

Alex looked out the window and watched as the cab traveled downtown along the FDR Highway. Looking to the left he could see Brooklyn across the East River. The cab was just about to go under the Williamsburg Bridge that crosses the river into Brooklyn. In the distance he could see the Brooklyn Bridge.

They all continued looking forward or out the side window, deep in their own thoughts. As the cab approached the Brooklyn Bridge. it turned right heading away from the river, leaving the highway and traveling across town on city streets. In the distance they could see the government buildings. They all looked the same, a style of their own… all nondescript limestone buildings. The cab turned onto Hogan Place and pulled over to the curb. They had arrived.

They got out of the cab, paid the driver, and watched as it drove away, turning to the right at the corner along Columbus Park. This park was known for many protests and marches during the Viet Nam war.

They stood there looking up at the tall building in front of them. It was constructed from yellow limestone and stood 16 floors high. It was just a rectangular government building, like all the buildings in the area

"Well" Alex said, "let's go and see what next adventure lies ahead of us."

Chapter 9

*T*he three of them entered the large lobby of the federal building with its polished marble floor. They walked to the reception desk, Alex taking the lead.

"We have an appointment with Lisa Fisher."

"Let me see some ID and please sign in" the armed guard stated pointing to a book on the desk.

Alex took the pen and signed in. He then handed the pen to Leslie while he retrieved his driver's license. After they had all signed in the guard called upstairs. "We have an Alex Gregory, Cindy Hudson, and Leslie Sherwood here who claim they have an appointment with Ms. Fisher" the guard said reading the names off the driver's licenses.

"Take the elevator to your right to the eighth floor. Ms. Fisher is in Suite 200, on the eighth floor" the guard explained as he handed back the licenses.

"Thank you."

They passed through x-ray machines to the elevator in silence, not knowing what to expect. Cindy pushed the elevator button and they waited. The elevator door opened, and they entered. They were the only people on this elevator. Alex pushed the button for the eighth floor and up they went, not stopping on any floor.

"Everyone ready" Alex asked as the elevator stopped, and the doors opened. He received nods from them.

They stepped out of the elevator into a long hallway with the same marble floors as in the lobby. In front of them was a door with a frosted glass insert in the center panel and the number 8-200 in black bold letters stenciled on the glass.

They walked into a room that screamed 'lawyer'. Leather chairs lined the wall with a picture of a judge in his robe, on the wall about each chair. A mahogany desk sat in the center of the room. A woman sat behind a desk working on a computer. File cabinets on the back wall behind the desk sat on either side of an entrance to a long hallway. At the end of the hall were windows looking at the building on the next block. Office doors opened into the hallway from each side. Several documents, some in blue binders, covered the desk of the receptionist.

"May I help you?" the perky brunette asked from behind the desk. She looked about 35, with short hair that hung straight down, ending about two inches above her shoulders. She wore a blue business suit with a white silk blouse, a bow at the neck. A blue jacket was carefully hung over the back of her chair. Her makeup was perfect, as if she had it professionally done.

Alex noticed a name plate on the corner of her desk...Marissa Weatherly. "We have an appointment with Ms. Fisher" Alex responded. "I'm Alex Gregory."

"Oh yes. Ms. Fisher has been expecting you." The receptionist was just about to pick up the phone when a woman appeared in the hallway, having exited from one of the many doors that open onto the hallway.

"Good afternoon, Mr. Gregory. I've been looking forward to meeting you. I'm Lisa Fisher."

She extended her had to Alex. She had a firm grip.

"I assume this is Cindy Hudson, and Leslie Sherwood. Let's move to a conference room where it is more comfortable." With that she turned and led the way down the hall to a small conference room at the end of the hall. There was a round mahogany table in the center of the room with the walls painted a light gray. Pictures of court houses were on the wall around the room. Two large windows on the outside wall looked out at another building about twelve feet away. A small refrigerator stood in the corner and a coffee machine on a counter next to it. At the other end of the counter was a large bottled water dispenser. Next to the coffee maker was a small sink with cupboards overhead.

"Please be seated. Would you care for something to drink... coffee, tea, water, or soda?"

"Nothing for me" Alex stated. The other two said the same.

"Thank you for coming by so quickly. I'm sorry I had to do it via a summons, but I had to make sure you were all contacted at the same time. I hope it didn't upset you in any way."

Lisa waited for a reaction. Not getting any, she continued.

"Do you mind if I tape our session?" Lisa asked as she placed a small recorder in front of her. "I don't want to miss anything and want to make sure that I understand everything that was said. I will make sure you each get a written transcript of what is said here if you request it. I will also need each of you to sign a confidentiality agreement as well."

"It is okay with me" Alex replied. Leslie and Cindy shook their heads in agreement. There was a click as the tape recorder was turned on.

"The case we will be discussing is the State of New York vs Tony Gianti, Rob Schimel, and Tony Neuman for the murder and murder for hire of Peter Hudson, Dawn Manning and Brianna Welch. This is Lisa Fisher from the District Attorney's office in Manhattan sitting with Alex Gregory, Cindy Hudson and Leslie

Sherwood. Do each of you understand the purpose of the meeting and are here of your own free will? Please state our name, date and respond either yes or no."

There was a yes confirmation from everyone, following by each providing the information requested.

"Now that the formalities are over, just talk casually as if the recording is not here. I will not be prosecuting the case. That will be done by Allison Markus, the Assistant District Attorney for New York. I am here to get the background facts and if Allison needs anything else, she will contact your directly."

She turned her attention to Alex.

"Alex, I understand you are the one who put this all together so let me start with you. Just tell me everything that happened."

Everyone looked at Alex.

"First of all, I want to say that all of us played a part in the discovery and worked together to put all the pieces together. It all started on my first day of work when I received a call from Cindy Hudson. I had no idea who she was. She called me several times and insisted that we meet to talk about her husband. Her husband had died of a heart attack while on a business trip and I was hired to fill the position he had at Sterling Chemicals. I decided to meet with her to hear about her husband and maybe get some insight about the job I was about to begin. That is where it all started."

"This is the same Peter Hudson as specified in the indictment. Is that correct?"

Both Alex and Cindy responded 'yes' at the same time.

"Anything else to add Cindy?" Lisa asked.

"No, Alex is covering everything."

"Please continue Alex."

Alex continued with all the details over the past several weeks. He described his meeting with Cindy and the file of documents that Peter had compiled about the new product that Sterling was about to market. Peter was sure that something was wrong with the product but couldn't put his finger on it. The product only had a number, 57162. It killed every crop pest on every plant it was applied, and at the same time increased the crop yield two to three times. It was a wonder pesticide for the food industry. It would make millions for Sterling the first year. The plans for the second year were to introduce it worldwide.

Alex continued describing how over the next three weeks the three of them found evidence that mosquitoes sprayed with the product did not die, but produced a small amount of pyrethroid compounds in their saliva, a chemical that is usually lethal to insects. It wasn't strong enough to kill the mosquito, but if a person was bitten by several mosquitos in a short period of time, it caused the person to show signs of pyrethroid poisoning. This could be fatal in small children or seniors. Alex had witnessed this when visiting the company's research farm in North Carolina.

"That is frightening. Go on Alex" Lisa said, her eyes fixed on Alex's face.

"We then suspected that we were being followed. Leslie was the first to notice the same person being at the same places we were. We later found out that his name was Tony Neuman. I thought it was just a coincidence, but Leslie was sure he was following us. We set up a test to see if he was following me and sure enough, she was right. Leslie had noticed him at the company cafeteria one day at lunch. I left the cafeteria, leaving Leslie behind. Leslie was to text me if he left right after me. Sure enough, he did. I went to a drug store down the street from the office and stood behind a shelf where I could not be seen, yet I could see anyone who entered the store. Within a few minutes, Tony entered the store. I was now convinced he was following me. But it all came to light when we met with Brianna several days later."

"What happened then?" Lisa asked.

"Brianna showed up one day at Leslie's. She had suspected something was going on but was not sure what it was. She also felt that we were in danger. Leslie and I had been invited by Tony Giani to join him on a company business trip to the chemical manufacturing plant in West Virginia. Brianna had never been invited to tour the plants or any business trip and had with the company for years. Leslie had only been with the company a few weeks and asked to go to the manufacturing plants, something that had nothing to do with her job. Brianna said she then thought of Peter and what happened to him on a business trip."

Alex looked at Cindy to see how she was doing. He noticed her eyes where a little moist.

Turning back to Lisa, Alex continued.

"Brianna had realized in her own way that something was wrong. Apparently, she had heard conversations between Mr. Gianti and Tony Neuman and put things together. Tony was a hired consultant, hired by Mr. Gianti. Brianna showed up at Leslie apartment one day to tell us of her suspicions and deliver some R&D documents and bank transfer evidence.

"What did you find in the documents?"

"There were studies by R&D that the plants that were sprayed by the new product started using oxygen, thus competing with animals for the air we breathe. There was no immediate effect but over generations it could potentially deplete our oxygen supply to wipe out the human population."

"Go on" Lisa said.

"The company was in deep financial debt and this new product was going to be the savior of the company. Peter suspected that something was wrong with this product. Tony Gianti could not let him find out how bad the product was affecting the environment. The company depended on that product to survive. Dawn had notice discrepancies in the financials with a bank in Miami. Peter had suddenly died of a heart attack, and Dawn disappeared shortly after Tony Neuman was hired.

"What about Brianna's death?"

"After Brianna left Leslie's apartment she was run down and killed by a hit and run. Leslie and I witnessed the accident from Leslie apartment window. We both noticed Tony Neuman standing in the background when the ambulance arrived. That was no accident. Now everything fell into place except one thing. She gave her life to save her friends and save the company she had worked her entire career."

"What was that?"

"There had to be a third person involved in the cover-up since Tony Neuman was at the scene of the accident and could not have been driving the car. With the help of Leslie's father, who is President of a Bank in Connecticut, the monies deposited in the bank in Florida had been transferred to Rob Schimel, an assistant to a Senior Vice President at Sterling. Four large deposits of $50,000 each had been deposited in Rob's account. It was murder for hire, authorized of Tony Gianti. Rob must have been driving the car. Four deposits, four deaths. Two had been for Dawn and Peter. Brianna has suspected the third and fourth transfer was for an accident to happen to Leslie and me on our trip to West Virginia. We now suspect that one of the payments was for her death.

"Go on please."

"That night the three of us disappeared and faked our own deaths. We staged an accident with a car I had rented so it could be traced back to me. The car accidentally went over the Palisades in New Jersey and disappeared into the Hudson River. The car was found but no bodies. It was therefore assumed that the bodies were washed out to sea by the strong currents."

"Yes, I saw all the stories in the papers and on the news."

"Prior to disappear, we had prepared an analysis of what we thought happened. That analysis along with the supporting documents from Sterling, were delivered to the Police and the New York Times."

"The Police contacted us the next day and we obtained a copy of everything they had" Lisa added. "Two days later, they arrested Tony Gianti, Tony Neuman and Rob Schimel. They are now siting at Riker's Island awaiting trial."

Alex looked at his watch. It was 5:45. They had been talking for three and a half hours. Leslie and Cindy helped fill in the gaps with Alex doing most of the talking. They had answered all of Lisa's questions too.

"Thank you, Alex, Leslie and Cindy for your input to this case and spending time here. It is late and I'm sure you wish to get home. If you think of anything else, please call." She handed each of them her business card with her direct number on it. "If I have any further questions, I will call Alex. Is that okay with you Alex?"

"Yes. Can you tell us what happens next?"

"With the information you have just provided, and the documents left with the police department, we hope to go in front of the Grand Jury soon. At that point, a trial date will be set. There is no doubt in our minds that there will be a trial."

"Will we be called to testify?" Leslie asked, her voice shaking.

"I can't guarantee at this time if all three of you will be called. But I'm sure that Alex will be called for the prosecution." She turned to Alex to get his reaction. There was none.

"You will be properly coached Alex when you testify. All you must do is tell the truth. We will help you through your testimony to makes sure that it is worded for the jury to understand. Are there any other questions?"

No one said anything. Lisa picked up her cell phone and dialed a number. "Thanks for staying this late Marissa. Please call the police department and have them send over a car to take these three people home. Then you can leave."

About 5 minutes later an officer in uniform appeared at the conference room door.

"Thank you for coming by" Lisa said to the officer standing the doorway. "Please take these three to their homes. They are part of an investigation and have been very helpful."

Lisa turned back to each of them, shook their hand and reaffirmed that everything will be okay. "Thank you for coming in today. I really appreciate it. You have been a great help, and this will all soon be behind you" Lisa said. "If you have any questions or concerns please feel free to call me on the number on the card". This officer will take you home."

"Please follow me" the officer said as he turned from the door and heading down the hallway toward the elevator. Alex led the way, as the three of them followed the policeman and Lisa returned to her office.

There was a black car sitting in front of the building in a no parking area. The office opened the door for them.

Alex sat in the front with the policeman, and Cindy and Leslie in the back. No one said a word. Everyone was in their own thoughts. Alex would have been excited about being in the police car if it were under better circumstances. He expected to find all types of electronic gadgets and a wall between the front and back seat. But it turned out to be a very ordinary car.

The policeman dropped Cindy off first. Alex moved into the back seat. He grabbed Leslie's hand and they looked into each other's eyes, neither one saying a word. Alex held her hand all the way to the next stop, his place. Since they were in Manhattan it was easier to drop him off before heading to Brooklyn to take Leslie home. Alex wanted to ride to Brooklyn with Leslie to make sure she got home safely, but she assured him that she would be okay, and that they both needed a good night's sleep.

"See you tomorrow" he said as he shut the car door. Standing in front of his apartment building, he watched the police car as it went to the end of the block and disappeared around the corner on its way to Brooklyn.

What a day, he thought. *And this is only the beginning.*

Chapter 10

*W*aking up early, Alex reached over and shut off the alarm clock. He just lay there, thinking about the day ahead. He felt anxious going back to work. This would be his first full day back since he went into hiding, presumed dead. It is going to be like his first day at work, without the new employee orientation meetings. He had no idea what he would be working on since the product he was evaluating had been pulled from further development.

He showered and dressed quickly, picked up his backpack and headed out the door. On Broadway he entered the subway entrance and stood on the platform with everyone else, waiting for the train to arrive. At Time Square he exited the subway station, out of the tunnel into the light, along with hundreds of other commuters. Heading toward the office he picked up coffee and a bagel from a street vendor. He entered the building for Sterling Chemicals, passed through security and took the elevator to the 42nd floor. His office was just as he left it yesterday. But it felt like his first day.

Sitting at his desk he took a bite from his bagel, and turned on his computer, taking a second bite while the computer booted up.

He had 52 emails waiting for him…many of them welcoming him back. Did they know where he had been and why? Several of the names he didn't even recognize. There were several from R&D asking if he had any updates on his analysis of 57162. They were emails from before the product was pulled from the market. There was one from Donna Holland from HR. It was sent yesterday. She had presided over the orientation meeting for all new employees on his first day of work, telling everyone the "dos and don'ts" of working at Sterling

Chemicals. She never smiled and her actions were very stoic, conveying the message that these orientation sessions were a waste of her time. Alex had given her the nickname "tight ass". Alex opened the email.

"Welcome back Dr. Gregory. I hope that your time away from the office was productive and that you are anxious to start your career with Sterling Chemicals. You exemplify what Sterling is all about. Once you are settled, please give me a call so we can arrange a meeting."

Now what is that about? Doesn't sound like her! Also, sounds like she knows why he was away.

"Are you starting again? Going to try a second time?

Alex looked up and saw his boss, Gene Mathews, standing in the doorway.

"I'm ready to go and try to get some normalcy back into my life... if it will ever be normal again."

Gene walked in, shut the door behind him and sat in the chair across from Alex.

"Really Alex, how are you doing? You have been through a lot in the last month. More than many people do in a lifetime."

"I'm doing okay. Thanks for asking. I must admit though, I never had any training for that, and it is something I hope I never have to do again. But I am concerned about Leslie and Cindy. They are trying to appear strong, but I know they are still scared."

"They are both strong women. They will be okay. And the three of you have each other to lean on"

"I hope you are right."

"I was very sad when I heard that news that you might have been dead. You had just started working here. I just wouldn't accept that idea, but everything pointed to that conclusion."

"I'm sorry sir that I didn't contact you and let you know I was safe. But at that point, none of us knew who we could trust. I hope you aren't upset over that?"

"Not at all. I don't know what I would have done under the circumstances, and hope I never have to find out."

"I wouldn't want anyone to go through that. I'm glad it is almost over. How and when did you find out the truth?"

"It all came to light the day the police showed up and escorted Mr. Gianti, Mr. Schimel and Mr. Neuman out of the building in handcuffs. It was thirty minutes later that Mr. Sterling called me to his office. When I got there, he was talking to the company's in-house lawyers. He told us everything that police told him, which I guess wasn't much. It was at that time that we were all sure that you were still alive, but in hiding... part of your plan to protect the three of you."

"I'm glad you found out early. I'm sorry to make you go through that. So. what is next? Anything you can tell me?"

"Mr. Sterling has asked me to move up to the 62nd floor and help him get the company back on track. He has hired a PR company to help raise consumer confidence. In my opinion Alex, you three saved the company from destruction...and we are all very thankful."

"Don't forget Peter Hudson. He had a major role in the discovery... and Dawn and Brianna.

"Yes, they were also part of the discovery and we are all in their debt."

"Congratulations on your promotion. Mr. Sterling already told me about it. I'm sure it is well deserved" Alex added not knowing what else to say.

"Thank you. I have asked Andrea Cushman to move in as acting marketing director as I move into my new role. She is the only other person in this department who knows of your involvement. However, once the trial starts it will all be in the open, so you need to be prepared for that. I've asked Donna Holland to help if you ever need someone to run interference for you. I know people think of her as being rigid; but in her position it is a necessity."

So that is the reason for her email.

"Thank you. It is good to know that there are resources here to help as this goes forward. I haven't had any time to really think about all the things that I might be facing."

"You three need to think about the next steps. Once the trial starts, your names will be all over the news and you need to be ready to respond to what may happen. You will be approached by people here at work as well as the news media. Donna can help with that."

"My name has already been leaked. I've been getting calls from reporters from all over the country."

"Then best you start working with Donna. She will be a great help, believe me."

"Thank you. Now that I am back, what products do you want me to review? My main emphasis, for the short time I was here, was on 57162."

"There are several new products in the pipeline. I've discussed these with Andrea, and we need to see if we have any potential new products to move to the next phase of development as we re-invent the company. Andrea will be contacting you as soon as you are ready and the two of you can then work out the next steps."

Gene looked at his watch. "I've asked Donna to meet us now. You two need to start working together. We have a lot of work to do. Better sooner than later. I'll meet you by the elevator in 5 minutes."

With that, Gene got up and left the office.

Alex turned back to his bagel and now cold coffee. Picking up the phone he dialed Leslie's number. He barely had time to make one phone call before he had to leave.

"How about lunch? I'll meet you in the cafeteria at 12:15."

"You will see me before that. I am just leaving to attend a meeting with HR. See you there."

Alex hung up the phone, pulled out a notebook and pen from his briefcase, finished his cold coffee and headed to the elevator. He saw Gene just arriving, a few seconds before him. He saw Gene pushed the UP bottom.

But HR was on the second floor. Why were they going up? he asked himself.

"We are meeting in a conference room on the 62nd floor so we are out of eyesight of other employees."

As the elevator door opened on the 62nd floor, Alex saw 'tight ass' sitting in a leather chair."

"I thought I would wait, and we would all go into together. Good to see you again Alex" Donna remarked, holding out her hand. "I remember you from the orientation."

"Good to see you again, Ms. Holland" he replied as he shook her hand.

She then told the guard at the reception desk that they were all here and ready to go to the conference room. The guard made a call to someone inside. The door opened, and they were led to a conference room. As they entered Alex saw Leslie sitting alone at the table. He immediately went over and took a seat next to her. It was a small conference room with only six chairs around a round table.

Alex leaned over to Leslie. "I decided to come up to the 62nd floor and see if it was good enough for you to work up here. I'll let you know later what I decide."

Leslie gave Alex a small hit on his arm and smiled.

"Thank you for coming Leslie. Donna remarked. "It's early in the morning and you all might want to get some coffee or tea before we start." Everyone got up, filled a cup and returned to the table.

Leslie and Alex sat together on one side of the table with Gene and Donna across facing them. Alex opened his notebook ready to take notes.

"Let's not take any notes about this meeting and what we discuss." Gene stated. "We don't want any notes lying around for others to see. That is how rumors start and why we decided to meet up here."

"We've never had an incident like this at Sterling" Donna started. "We are in new territory. Just so we are all on the same page, I'm referring to the arrests of Mr. Gianti, Mr. Schimel and Mr. Neuman and their involvement in the deaths of Donna Manning, Brianna Welch, and Dr. Peter Hudson. I thought it best that we have an open discussion and develop some ground rules so we are all on the same page. First, have either of you been approached or contacted by the police or media?"

"Leslie, Cindy and I were at the district attorney's office yesterday and answered all their questions."

"Alex did most of the talking. Cindy and I were there to provide additional information needed."

"How do you feel about your experience there?" Donna asked.

"It was my first time talking to an attorney. In the back of my mind, I knew our testimony would be needed at some point in time. Yesterday it all came true. They advised us not to talk to anyone, especially the press" Alex said.

"Has the press contacted you? Donna asked.

"I have had calls from the media as far away as Chicago" Alex started. "My answering machine was full when I returned to my apartment after being away. Since then I've disconnected the machine."

"And what did they want."

"They want my take on the situation here."

"And how did you answer them."

"I just hung up on them."

"Do you have any idea how they found you?" Gene asked.

"My guess is that they found the courier service I used to deliver the documents to the police."

"What about you Leslie, any phone calls?" Gene asked.

"I haven't received any calls."

"I haven't seen our names on TV so far" Alex added. "The District Attorney told us there was a gag order on the media not to release our names."

"It won't be long before everyone will hear your names, so let's be prepared" Gene interjected "especially once they are arraigned, which should happen any day now."

"Here is what I suggest." Donna said. "Any call you get from the media, respond with 'no comment' and hang up. If you have call waiting, don't answer any number you don't recognize. If anyone approaches you on the street also respond with 'no comments and continue walking answering no questions. If someone comes to your apartment don't let them in. Do you have security at your building?"

"I have a doorman, and everyone has to be announced so no one can theoretically get up to my place without me knowing." Alex responded. People have been known to sneak in behind someone else or get let in by another resident. That doesn't happen often though. No one will be able to talk to me that I don't want to talk to so I'm okay."

"I don't have a doorman in my building, but no one can get in without me buzzing them in. I think that will be enough" Leslie said.

"What about people at work. What do we tell them?" Alex asked?

"I will take care of that" Gene added. "Donna I will put out a note to all employees in this building that the trial is not to be discussed with anyone inside or outside of the company. And if someone does talk to you, just tell them that everyone has been instructed not to talk about the trial or anything related to it. And if anyone persists, you are to let Donna know as soon as possible and we will handle it."

"What about Cindy?" Leslie asked?

"I've talked to her and she told me she hasn't had any phone calls. I gave her the same instructions that I gave you…no comment" Donna added. "But that is all I know about her situation at this time. We will also continue to work with her as if she is one of the employees. She says she is okay with that arrangement."

"I suggest that we invite her to the office and the five of us go over our ideas with her" Gene suggested. "That will be a good review for all of us, as well as a chance to discuss any issues we might think of between now and then? Mr. Sterling has asked me to be a contact for you three when needed" Gene added, looking first at Alex and then Leslie. "However, Ms. Holland should be your first contact for questions."

"I think a meeting is a good idea" Alex stated. "Do you want me to call Cindy and set up a meeting?"

"I will contact her" Donna said. "Does everyone agree with that?"

"I would let Alex call, if it is okay with everyone" Leslie added. "Cindy trusts him and if I can be honest, I don't know how she feels about this company after what happened to her husband while he worked here" Leslie added.

"I agree with Leslie" Gene added. "Thanks Alex, for offering to call her. Please set this up as soon as possible."

"I'll call her this afternoon and let you all know."

"I've set up a secure web site that only the four of us and Cindy will have access. It is here you can record ideas, thoughts, ask questions or anything you want to share with the group. You can also use the phone. If you do use the phone to talk to each other about this case, make sure no one is around within hearing distance. I suggest closed door discussions" Gene remarked.

"Aren't you afraid of hackers on the website?" Leslie asked. "Afterall you hear about that all the time on the news."

"I don't think there will be anything of importance to anyone else but this small group. There are no company secrets. I just want a place for each of you to document your thoughts, ideas, things you remember for all to have access. I don't like the idea of thoughts being on scraps of paper that could get misunderstood that could lead to rumors getting started."

"Good idea" Alex added.

Reaching into his pocket Gene pulled out three 3x5 index cards and passed one to each of them. "On the card is the website log-in procedures. When you go there the first time it will ask you for the code listed on the card. The code can only be used once. When you get into the system you will be asked to enter the last 4 digits of your Social Security Number. Then it will pull up a screen for you to enter an ID and password. Once you have registered, shred the card. Any questions?"

Everyone was looking at the cards.

"If there aren't any further questions we are done here" Gene said. "Almost time for lunch anyway."

With that they all got up to leave. Alex turned to Leslie and quietly said "stay behind."

After Donna and Gene left Alex turned to Leslie. "You are more than welcome to stay with me if you want during the trial. We can go to work together."

"That is sweet of you Alex, but I will be okay. I will keep the offer close to my heart and if need so, take you up on it."

"You know you have an open offer to stay at my place anytime. Even after the trail." Alex said with wink. "Now let's go to lunch. All I had for breakfast was a bagel and I'm hungry." Again, he wanted to take her in his arms and hold her tight but knew it was not the time and place. He could only dream how she would feel in his arms.

Chapter 11

*T*he rest of the day went by quickly and Alex was ready to get home. He walked to the subway and waited on the platform for the number 2 or 3 train to take him to the Upper West Side. The train arrived and he pushed his way into the subway car with all the other commuters heading home. All the seats were taken so he stood elbow to elbow with all the other passengers heading uptown, pushed together like sardines. People around him were on their iPhones, texting, reading, or playing games, anything to pass the time…a typical subway distraction.

How many years will I be doing this? he thought.

While standing, Alex thought about everything that had happened in the last couple of days. Maybe now he can get back to his career and the reasons he accepted this job. The only thing in the way to normalcy now was the pending trial. He hoped that would get over quickly. Something told him that it would not be a short trial. Afterall, Mr. Gianti was wealthy and could hire the best lawyers to get the trial delayed. Maybe his part would get over quickly.

He wasn't looking forward to being called to testify. He pictured himself in front of the lawyers and jury being drilled repeatedly, like they do on television. The district attorney assured him that television is all drama and it is not like that at all in the court room. He just had to tell his side of the story. She also assured him that she would help him through the process.

The subway pulled into the 96th street stop, and Alex pushed his way out on to the platform. He moved up the stairs to the street level with the other commuters exiting in his neighborhood. He stopped at the bodega on the corner to pick up something for dinner, and then walked the two short blocks to his apartment.

Entering his apartment, he threw his keys on the table by the door and dropped his knapsack by the door, really to be picked up tomorrow on his way out. Kicking off his shoes, he headed to the kitchen, got a cold beer from the refrigerator, and moved to the sofa. Putting his feet up on the coffee table, he turned on the TV to watch the news. Glancing over at his phone he noticed that the message button was flashing. He had decided to plug it back in yet screen his calls. He'd listen to them later. Right now, he just wanted to enjoy his beer and watch the news.

"It was a beautiful day here in New York" the weatherman reported "and it looks like it will be the same tomorrow. We are expecting a clear day, with a high of 82. A perfect day to enjoy a day outside. We'll see...."

Just then the program was interrupted with an important bulletin. "We just learned that Tony Neuman has escaped while being transferred to the courthouse this afternoon. Tony Neuman is on trial for the murder for hire of three people at Sterling Chemicals. Mr. Neuman was able to overpower two policemen and escape. He jumped into a car and sped away. We don't know if the car was waiting for him or if he hijacked it in his escape. All we know is that he got into the car on the passenger side. Mr. Neuman is dangerous. If you see him, please contact the police at the number listed. Do not try to apprehend him. We will keep you informed as more information becomes available. Now back to our regularly scheduled program." Tony Neuman's picture was flashed across the screen. It brought chills to Alex.

Alex just sat there and stared at the television, not aware of anything around him. The phone rang and it broke his trance.

Maybe that is Leslie calling he thought as he raced to the phone. "Hello, Leslie?"

"Mr. Gregory?" was all he heard from the phone

"Yes?"

"This is Allison Markus from the District Attorney's Office. I'm calling you regarding an incident that happened in the past thirty minutes. Mr. Neuman...."

"I already heard the news broadcast if that is what you are talking about" Alex interrupted.

"Yes, that is why I am calling. I have been trying to reach you, Leslie and Cindy for past half hour. I got hold of Cindy but haven't been able to reach Leslie yet. I was hoping she might be with you."

"No, she is not here. She should be at home soon. She is probably still on the subway. Do you have her home number?" That was a silly question; of course, she has Leslie's number.

"I will continue to call her. I am sending a policeman as a precaution to your apartment building as well as Cindy's and Leslie's apartments. They will be there for your safety."

Just then there was a knock on his door. It must be the police since the doorman did not call up to announce a visitor.

"I think he is here now. Someone just knocked on my door."

"Just be careful the next couple of days. I'll talk to you soon. Thank you Mr. Gregory, and don't worry."

Don't worry. Easier said than done Alex thought.

Alex opened his door to find a uniformed policeman standing there holding his cap in his hands. He was over 6 feet tall, in his mid-thirties, brown hair cut short, face with a square jaw and appeared to be in good physical shape.

"Mr. Gregory? I'm Officer Martini. I have been assigned to you from the District Attorney's Office. Just go on your normal business. You won't know I'm here. Just let me know if you plan on leaving the building. Here is my card and phone number" he said handing Alex his contact card.

With that, the officer turned and headed toward the elevator.

"Wait Officer" he yelled, probably louder than he needed. "I need to go make sure that someone is okay. She lives in Brooklyn. She is also having a policeman assigned to her. I just want to make sure she is okay."

"Let me take you there, sir."

Alex grabbed his keys, locked the apartment, and joined the officer at the elevator.

If Leslie saw the bulletin, she must be terrified. Where is she? The lawyer said she has been calling and no answer. Leslie told him that she was going right home after work. She should be there by now. Her commute is shorter than his.

All types of thoughts went through Alex's head. He couldn't remember getting into the police car. The officer put on his siren whenever they ran into traffic. Alex didn't remember racing through the city. He was so concerned about Leslie. Alex tried to call her from the police car, but there was no answer.

Where was she?

Again, he called…still no answer. Looking out the window he noticed they were crossing the Brooklyn Bridge. Just five minutes away. Alex could feel sweat mounting on his forehead. *Please be okay Leslie,* is all he could think, as they exited off the Brooklyn Bridge.

Just six more blocks and they would be there. As they rounded the corner, he could see her building down the street. He already has his hand on the door handle, ready to leap out.

Chapter 12

*A*lex had the police car door open before it stopped at the curb. Mrs. Sester was standing on the steps of the brownstone with her key in her hand just entering the building, a shopping bag in her hand.

As he exited the police car, he noticed a similar car parked down the street and the figure of a man sitting in the driver's seat. He felt a sign of relief, thinking that might be the policeman assigned to watch Leslie. But he still wanted to make sure she was okay.

"So nice to see you again, Mrs. Sester" he remarked as he caught the door behind her and followed her in. "I don't have time to talk right now. Um, Leslie is having a problem with a leak and I need to fix it before it floods her apartment."

"Good to see you again Alex. I hope you get the leak fixed. Say hello to Leslie."

"I will" he responded as he moved around Mrs. Sester and raced up the stairs to the second floor, taking two steps at a time. Mrs. Sester lived across the hall from Leslie and was like a mother figure to her. She had hidden some documents in her apartment that were important in the arrest of the Sterling trio, the documents provided by Brianna. Leslie was afraid to leave them in her apartment in case of a break in... which there was.

As Alex reached the top of the stairs, he noticed that the door to Leslie apartment was open a bit. He pushed it open further and looked in.

Leslie was sitting on her sofa staring at a sheet of paper on her lap, her hand grasping it tightly. She didn't even look up as Alex entered the room. Alex walked slowly over to the sofa so as not to frighten her and sat down next to her, placing his hand on hers. Leslie turned her head to look at him. It was a blank stare, as if she was looking right through Alex, or didn't even register that he was sitting next to her.

"What's wrong Leslie? Are you okay?" is all he could say.

Leslie then realized that Alex was in the room. She blinked and looked into his eyes, at the same time closing the piece of paper she was holding tightly in her hands.

"Alex, I'm so scared? What is going on?"

"You are safe Leslie. There is a policeman outside who will be watching this place to make sure you are okay."

"Policeman? What are you talking about Alex?"

"Didn't the district attorney's office call you?"

Leslie turned and stared back at the piece of paper in her hand, still grasping it tightly.

Leslie didn't seem herself to Alex. She just wasn't her happy self. *Maybe she saw the news on the TV and that is the reason for her reaction.*

"Have you been watching television and heard the news bulletin?"

"No, I haven't had the TV on. I have been working around the apartment trying to get things back in order. Why, was something on about the case?"

"Did you get a call from the District Attorney's office?"

"The phone rang several times, but I didn't answer it."

Alex squeezed Leslie's hand tighter, so she knew he was there for her.

"I had just gotten home from work and was sitting and relaxing watching television" Alex continued. "A news bulletin flashed across the screen about the case. They were taking Tony Neuman to the courthouse and somehow he escaped and got away. So far they have no idea where he is."

Alex suspected some type of reaction from Leslie, but there was none. It was as if she was someplace else. She continued to look at the folded paper in her lap.

"The District Attorney's office called me and said they have assigned a police officer to watch the three of us until they determine we are in no danger."

"Okay" is all she said.

"I noticed a car with a policeman in it outside your apartment when I got here. Probably the police assigned to watch over you."

Still no reaction.

"I haven't talked to Cindy yet but I'm sure she is doing okay. I just wanted to make sure that you are okay." It was as if he was talking to thin air. There was no reaction from her.

"I'm fine. Thank you for your concern Alex" she said as she turned back to him.

But still no reaction or emotion.

Alex heard a quiet knock at the front door. Alex hadn't shut the door after he entered.

"Did you get the leak fixed Alex?" Mrs. Sester was standing in the doorway.

"False alarm" Alex responded. "Thank you for your concern."

"I had a leak in my kitchen about a year ago and it flooded the entire room. I didn't want that to happen to you. It was a real mess."

"I am glad we didn't have that" Alex added.

"Oh, I see you got the note I put under your door earlier Leslie. A woman was at the front door when I was leaving. She wanted to know which apartment you lived in. She wanted to leave you a note. Since I didn't know her, I told her I'd give you the note. She handed it to me and left quickly without a word. I knocked on your door, but you didn't answer. You must have been out, so I slipped it under the door. Is everything okay dear?"

"Yes, everything is fine. Thank you. I'll talk to you later" Leslie responded. Still no emotion in her voice.

"I'm glad there is no water problem. I'll go and leave you two alone" she said. She turned and left, closing the door behind her.

Leslie turned back to Alex. "Oh, hi Alex" she said, as if she just realized that he was in the room.

"Is something wrong? You don't seem yourself."

With that, Leslie looked down at the piece of paper she was clutching in her hand.

Alex's eyes followed Leslie's to the piece of paper.

"What's on the paper Leslie? Does it have something to do with this case?"

"Huh?..... No, it is something else."

"Something is bothering you. What can I do to help?"

Leslie slowly turned to Alex, and then back to the piece of paper she was holding.

"No, everything is fine."

Then slowly and with a soft voice she said, "No everything is not fine." She slowly turned back and looked at Alex, her eyes empty yet moist.

Alex saw a look of despair on her face, something he had never seen in her.

"What's wrong Leslie? Is there anything I can do to help?" he repeated.

"I don't know what to do?"

Tears start to appear in Leslies eyes, and one tear drop started to roll down here face…then another and another.

Alex put his arms around her and pulled her close to him, hoping to make her feel safe.

Has Tony gotten to her? Or someone else from the Sterling trial?

"Everything will be OK, Leslie. I'm here." As he held her, he felt her start to tremble and burst into sobs. Alex just held her tighter not knowing what to say.

Chapter 13

*A*lex held Leslie tightly until the sobbing stopped and she started to pull away. He didn't know what to say so he waited for her to tell him when she was ready.

Leslie slowly handed the piece of paper to Alex, not saying a word, only staring at him.

Alex opened the note and read it.

YOUR DAUGHTER SARA NEEDS YOU!

Nothing else, just those five words. Alex looked at it again to make sure he was reading it incorrectly. He turned it over and looked at the other side…nothing there.

Leslie was still looking at him, her hands tightly clutched together.

"What does this mean?" Alex asked. "You have a daughter?"

"I don't know" Leslie responded.

Alex continued to look at her, not understanding her response. *How would she not know?*

Leslie took a deep breath, wiped the tears from her cheek and looked seriously into Alex's eyes.

"Let me try to explain. I'm not sure I understand myself."

Alex waited.

"Here goes." Deep breath. "Ten years ago, I was walking home from a high school ball game. It was about ten pm. I was 17 years old and a senior in high school. It was dark and I was alone on the street. There weren't a lot of houses, just small business that were closed for the day. I had walked this street many times to and from school and felt perfectly safe."

Leslie looked away from Alex, as if looking for the right words to continue. Alex sat there waiting. It was a long wait.

Leslie looked back at him with a strange look on her face. Alex didn't know how to interpret that look.

"A guy came up behind me, threw a hood over my head and pushed me into the back of his van and raped me. He then pushed me out of the van and left. I never saw him or his van. I was too frightened to remove the hood. Eventually I did and found myself all alone on the street."

Silence…the strange look left her face to be replaced by a look of relief.

"I have never told anyone about this in ten years. I've wanted to tell you but was afraid. Afraid of what you might would think of me."

Alex put his arms around her and pulled her into his chest, holding her tightly.

Alex turned his mouth to her ear, "I only love you more for telling me and confiding in me. Never, never be afraid to tell me anything."

Leslie slowly pulled away and looked at him, tears in her eyes, rolling down her cheek.

"There is more" she said

Alex waited,

"I didn't tell my parents because I was so ashamed. I just wanted to put it behind me, hoping it would go away. But then I missed my period and I started to worry. After being two weeks late, I went to the doctor one day after school and found out that I was pregnant."

Alex could feel Leslie looking at him, looking for some sign of disappointment.

"Leslie, it was not your fault. Nothing has changed with me. Tell me the rest. I think you need to and want to."

"Yes" she responded softly.

"I had to tell my parents. It was hard thing to do, but I had to. I was afraid of what they would think. They just sat there and listened. I couldn't tell if they were sad, angry, or upset. They just listened. When I was finished, I know I was crying. I could feel the tears on my cheeks. My father got up from his chair, walked over to me and hugged me for the longest time. All he said was 'it was not your fault. We love you and we will get through this together.'"

"Knowing your parents as I know them, I would have expected that response. Leslie, they love you so much, it is so evident when I see them around you."

"My father took me to the police to file a report and then we waited. The man and van were never found."

"It was at the end of the school year, so I continued school and finished before my pregnancy started to show. "

"I assume you decided to keep the baby?"

"Yes and no. I don't believe in abortion and I felt this child needed a chance to grow up and experience life. So, I decided to give the baby up for adoption so it would have a nice home and a family."

Alex just sat there looking at Leslie, not knowing what to say. He hoped she could see that he really cared for her and was there for her.

"I postponed going to college until the winter semester. I spent the summer and fall at our lake cabin in Massachusetts to keep out of sight of our neighbors and friends. During that time, we worked in confidence with adoption agencies and found the perfect family for Sara. My father made all the arrangements and made sure everything was legal and would remain confidential. I never got a chance to really get to know the adopting parents. I did meet them but for only a very short time. On paper they sounded perfect. My parents spent lots of time investigating and meeting them, and they agreed that the baby would have a good life in a caring and loving home. For some reason they felt it best that I didn't get to know the couple. I just went along with it. I know very little about them. I can't even remember their names."

"That had to be terrible for you."

"It was. I kept thinking I wanted to keep the baby. But then, I knew that she deserved a home with two parents. So, it came down to what was best for the baby, not what I wanted. It was the hardest thing I ever had to do. I remember signing the papers and then crying."

Alex reached over and grabbed Leslie's hand.

"I went into labor in December. I had just turned eighteen in October. The baby's birthday would have been December 9th."

"What do you mean, 'would have been'" Alex asked.

"That is the date of the baby's brith. There were complications with the birth, so they had to put me out. When I woke up my father was sitting next to the bed holding my hand. He told me that the baby didn't make it."

"I'm so sorry" is all Alex could say.

"I remember crying for a long time and feeling so empty. My parents stayed with me. I never saw the baby or had a chance to hold her. My parents convinced me that was for the best. I only know it was a girl. I even named her Sara. Eventually I accepted it. Now ten years later, this note." Leslie looked at the note still in his hand. Leslie then turned back to Alex, looking for some type of reaction.

"I can see why you were upset from this note. This note sounds like Sara is alive… and needs you."

"No one but my parents and the people at the hospital knew I was pregnant. I was told that my baby died. So how could this be my daughter? And how did they know the name Sara? The only people who know that name and the spelling were my parents and the people at the hospital."

"I'm sure the baby's name was on the crib in the nursery, so anyone going in and out would know the name."

"You're right."

"So many questions Leslie. We don't need to answer them now. "But I need to know and find out what this note means."

Silence…

"Ok, if you are up to talking about it, let's look at some scenarios."

"Yes, I'm up for it."

More silence, Alex putting his thought together, not wanting to upset Leslie any more.

"I'm so glad I told you. I have wanted to tell you for so long but wasn't sure how you would take it. Thanks for listening and not disappearing, and more important not judging."

"First of all, Leslie…this doesn't change how I feel about you. In fact, I feel special in that you told me and no one else after a ten-year secret."

"Thank you" is all she could say with the twinkle back in her eye showing through the tears. "So, what are you thinking?"

"Okay…two scenarios come to mind. First, there is no child, and someone is playing a cruel joke on you or trying to upset or frighten you. Secondly, the baby was given to the adopting family. Your father just wanted to protect you so you could get on with your life and not have to worry. He did this by telling you that the baby had died. From what I know of your dad in the short time that I've gotten to know him, I think he would do anything to protect you."

"This goes beyond just taking care of me. But we have no secrets, so it is not in his character."

"This is bigger than a secret Leslie. He was protecting you from yourself."

"If he did place Sara with the adopting parents, it must be eating him up not to tell me. He knew I was going to put the baby up for adoption anyway and he was just carrying out my wishes…putting my feelings before his. So that doesn't make sense either; it is not in his character."

"It makes perfect sense to me. You had selected the family and completed all the documents. He was just carrying out your wishes, not thinking about the fact he was losing a grandchild. He wanted to make sure you could have a normal life and not worry about what happened to Sara. Therefore, the death story was a perfect solution. The only person who it hurt day after day was him."

"What he must be going through all these years."

"If this was the scenario, do you think your mom knew too?"

"I don't think mom knew. She would not have been able to keep it a secret. My father would have handled it all. But with all the people around I can't imagine how he could have carried it out."

"Your father is very resourceful when it comes to his family Leslie."

"Let's go back to the first scenario…the baby did die." Alex continued. "Is there anyone that you can think of that knew you were pregnant that might want to get back at you or your family? I would tend to think it is someone who wants to get back at you since the note was sent to you. If they wanted to get back at your dad, they would have sent a note to him."

"Maybe they did?"

"I think this note was meant for you Leslie" Alex responded.

"Not many knew I was pregnant. My parents rushed me off to their mountain cabin right after high school and I never went out in public while there, so no one around knew I was pregnant. Basically, only the nurses and family doctor when I went into the hospital. They are all friends of the family and I'm sure none of them would have sent a note to frighten me. And, while in the hospital I was totally isolated from anyone else. Only my parents knew the baby's name. That is what bothers me. That whoever sent this note knew the name I gave to the baby and that I spelled it without the 'h'."

"I wonder if there is a way we could find out if your dad got a note too. That way we would know for sure if the note was aimed at you or the entire family."

"If my father gets a note, he will be anxious to find out if I also got one. We just need to wait and see if I get a call."

Alex thought for a while. "Then let's think about the second scenario, that Sara is alive and needs your help." It was strange how easily the name rolled off his tongue, as if she was a real person.

The look on Leslie's face showed that she realized for the first time that her daughter may be alive.

"Oh My God!" is all she could say and started to tremble. "Could it be true. and Sara might be alive out there someplace?"

Alex moved in and took her in his arms. They have been sitting on the sofa since he entered the apartment. Several minutes went by before she pulled back.

"Are you okay Leslie?"

"This is all so unreal Alex. What is going on?"

"I don't know Leslie, but we will find out."

More silence.

"If Sara is alive and was placed up for adoption, your father would know where she is."

"Why do you think that Alex?"

"First of all, your father would have controlled every aspect of the adoption, one of which would be to know where the baby was placed. He knew that is what you wanted, but that was his grandchild. He would want nothing to happen to her. Also, he was one of three people who know that you named her Sara. He probably told the adoptive parents and they kept the name. My bet is that if she is alive, she is with the adoptive parents who you selected, and your father knows where she is. He has probably watched her grow up from afar all these years."

"Oh, Alex…do you really think it is possible and Sara is alive and needs me."

"Yes, Leslie. I do believe that is the better of the two choices. The only thing that bothers me with this idea is that if Sara is in trouble your father would surely know about it and would take care of it. So why does she need you?"

"What do we do Alex?"

"Do you remember the name of the adoptive parents that you had selected? We could track them down and see if they have a child ten years old named Sara. Maybe someone close to them sent the note to get back at you."

"I only met them briefly and now I can't remember their names. I think the only time I ever saw the name was on the release form I signed.

I was so upset that it didn't register in my mind. My father handled everything after that."

"Also, let's talk to Mrs. Sester and see what she remembers about the woman who left the note. Maybe we can get a description of the person. It might trigger something in your memory. Is it too late to go see her or should we wait until tomorrow? Most important however, are you up to it? But we should do it as soon as possible while it is still fresh in her memory."

"Yes…. let's do it. I must know what is going on. I can't wait until tomorrow. And Mrs. Sester won't mind us stopping by now."

Chapter 14

"*W*ho is it?" Mrs. Sester asked from the other side of the door.

"It's Leslie from across the hall."

They heard a click as the door was unlocked and open slightly. They saw Mrs. Sester's face through the small opening in the door. "You can't be too careful these days" she replied and opened the door all the way.

"We would like to ask you some questions about the person who left the note with you earlier."

"Come on in dear. I was just having a cup of tea. Please join me."

They both entered the living room, standing by the door waiting for instructions.

"Please sit while I get some more tea."

She disappeared into the kitchen while Alex and Leslie moved to the sofa and sat down. The apartment was a reversed replica of Leslie's, except the furniture and décor was twenty years older. The living room was painted a warm gray with one accent wall of burnt orange. In the center of that wall was an entertainment unit with a television that dominated the unit. Books and different figurines and vases were placed on the shelves that were part of the unit. The coffee table and end tables by the sofa were a dark wood. Matching tall lamps of brass and glass with a round shade were in the center of each end table. Wall to wall carpet covered the floor in a buff color. The front windows had sheer curtains with swags across the top that matched the carpeting.

"Here we are" Mrs. Sester said as she entered the room carrying a tray with a tea pot, 3 cups, sugar, and cream.

"Let me help you" Alex said as he got up and took the tray from her and set it on the coffee table in front of the sofa.

Mrs. Sester stood about 5'6" and was very slim…almost too thin. Her gray hair was tied back in a bun. Her cheeks were rosy, and her green eyes seemed to smile. The few times that Alex had talked to her she seemed to exude a sense of happiness. She wore a flower print dress with a simple collar and fluffy blue slippers on her feet. Alex estimated her age to be in her mid-sixties.

"Help yourself to tea. I have some cookies in the kitchen. I'm sorry, but that is all I have."

"Don't worry about any food. Tea is perfect. It was so nice of you to invite us in at this hour."

"It's not that late, I'm a night owl anyway. I'm so glad you didn't have a water leak. They can be so messy. I had one once and it took weeks for everything to dry out."

Leslie looked at Alex with a questioning look on her face.

"Yes, I'm glad that it was a false alarm. Leslie heard some noises in the pipes and was concerned that it might be a lead so called me."

"That happens all the time in a building this old" Mrs. Sester responded.

"Yes, I was glad there was no leak" Leslie added, not knowing what they were talking about, hoping her comment fit in the conversation.

"I just noticed that your apartment seems to have the same layout as Leslie's." Alex wanted to have a casual conversion before he approached the reason for their visit.

"That is the way these brownstones were built. Mirror images on the second floor with the stairs and hallway dividing the two sides. I think Leslie's apartment must have been the master bedroom since she has a fireplace. This brownstone was made into four apartments in the fifties. Before that, it was a private house."

"I like your accent wall" Alex added pointing to the orange wall. "It adds a new dimension to the room. I especially like the color."

"It was my husband's idea. One day he just got up, went to the store, bought the paint, and painted it in one day. Didn't even ask for my opinion. I keep it there in memory of him. Every time I look at it, I think of him. He has been gone now for seven years and I still miss him."

"I'm sorry" Alex responded.

"Thank you dear."

How long have you lived here?" Alex asked.

"About twenty years. Seems like yesterday. Time seems to go by so fast the older you get."

Alex looked at Leslie. She seemed anxious. He knew she wanted to get to the reason for their stopping by.

"Have some more tea dear" Mrs. Sester said, noticing that Leslie's cup was empty. "I can make some more" she added as she started to get up.

"No thank you" Leslie responded "I've had quit enough. The caffeine will keep me awake tonight."

"I can drink tea all day and sleep like a baby at night. Staying awake is my problem" Mrs. Sester responded.

Alex felt the time was right. He looked at Leslie and gave her a wink to start the conversation about the note. They had set up this signal earlier.

"Thank you again for delivering the note to me. I really appreciate it."

"It was no trouble. The young woman didn't know where you lived. And I didn't want to send a stranger to your apartment. I hope it was okay for me to take the note."

"It was fine. Thank you again."

"So, you didn't recognize the woman?" Alex asked.

"No, I had never seen her before. Did you know her Leslie?"

"She didn't leave a name or phone number on the note, so I have no idea of who she is. Did she give you a name?"

"She didn't say anything. Just wanted to know what apartment yours was. That seemed strange to me. If she knew the building, you would expect she knew which apartment you lived in. That struck me strange and that is why I didn't tell her. Did I do something wrong?"

"No, you did nothing wrong" Leslie quickly interjected."

"Can you tell us how you ran into her? Maybe that will help Leslie try to figure out who she was" Alex asked.

"Well I was just going out to the corner store to get some butter and baking potatoes. I was in the mood for a baked potato and realized I didn't have any. So, I thought I would get one for dinner. I hadn't been out of the apartment all day, so the fresh air was nice. As you know, the store is only at the end of the block across the street, so it was an easy trip."

"Yes, it is nice to have it so close" Leslie added.

"Anyway, as I was going out, she was coming up the stairs. She didn't look at me but kept her head down. She asked if you lived here. I got suspicious when she didn't look at me. I asked her what she wanted so she would look at me."

"When I said you lived here, she asked for the apartment number. She said she had a note to give to you. I told her to give it to me and I would make sure that you got it. She gave it to me and then turned and hurried off as if someone were chasing her."

"Can you describe her?" Leslie asked.

"It was hard to see her since she kept her head down and was wearing one of those shirts that had a hood. It was pulled up over her head and down across her forehead. It is as if she didn't want anyone to recognize her."

"Tell us anything you remember and maybe we can figure out who she is" Alex asked.

"I know she was a white woman and from the veins in her hands I would say she was in her forties. When you get older you start guessing a person's age by the wrinkles on the back of their hands. With all the plastic surgery today, you can't go by a person's face. All the TV and movie people look a lot younger than they really are. Check the back of their hands sometimes."

"Anything else?"

She also had red hair. It was so red that I'm sure that it was out of a bottle. Her hair about shoulder length. She was very slim, about like you Leslie, except maybe taller. I watched her move quickly to the end of the block and around the corner, never looking back. Does that help dear?"

"That helps very much. I know that woman. She used to work with me at the bank" Leslie remarked." She just went through a bad divorce and that is probably why she was in such a hurry. Thank you for getting the note to me."

"I'm so glad I could be of help. I just didn't want to do anything wrong."

"I appreciate what you did…everything you have done for me. And we better go. I have some things to do before tomorrow and Alex needs to get back to the city. And thank you for the tea."

With that Leslie and Alex stood up.

"I hope it doesn't keep you up dear."

"Let me carry that back to the kitchen for you" Alex offered

"No need, I can take care of it myself. As you know, New York kitchens are small, and I know where everything goes."

Mrs. Sester walked them the short distance to the door. As they left, she added "I'm so glad it all worked out."

After they entered Leslie's apartment and the door shut behind them, Alex turned to Leslie.

"Now we know it is someone you used to work with. That will make it easy to track down. Or…were you just saying that so we could leave?"

Leslie looked straight into Alex's eyes.

"I haven't the slightest idea who that person is. I just said that so Mrs. Sester would feed better. We are back to square one."

"You go pack a bag. You are coming to stay with me for a couple of days or until I feel you can be left alone. No questions."

"I'll agree to that" Leslie responded. She got up and went into the bedroom. Alex could hear drawers opening and closing. He sat and waited, thinking about everything that has happened in the last twenty-four hours.

"Okay, I'm ready,

Alex walked took the suitcase from her and opened the front door. They walked down the stairs in silence, down the front steps of the building and over to the police car that was still parked by the curve. They got in the back seat. The car pulled out and the other police car pulled out behind them as they heading to the Alex's place.

No one noticed the black SUV parked at the opposite end of the block with two men sitting in it. The passenger was turned around watching the police leave in the opposite direction from them. The driver was watching through the rear-view mirror. He was wearing a blue shirt. Tony Neuman watched the police car turn the corner. A smirk was on his face.

Chapter 15

*I*t was a sleepless night for Alex. Leslie tossed and turned throughout the night. He tried to hold her tightly, but it was a losing battle. Several times he woke up and found her crying. Morning finally came and they had to get up to go to work. Alex woke up first and gently slid out of the bed to let Leslie sleep. She looked so peaceful now. It had been a rough night.

Moving quietly into the kitchen, he put on the coffee and just stood there smelling the aroma as the hot water dripped over the grounds.

"I hope you are making enough for two."

"Of course, several cups for each of us" he said, turning and seeing Leslie standing in the doorway.

"Smells so good…it woke me up. You can make coffee for me any morning."

"I'll hold you to that" he said, walking over to her and putting his arms around her.

"Good morning Alex."

"Good morning. You had a rough night. I'm sure you didn't have a good rest. How are you feeling this morning?"

"As if I could sleep twelve more hours. But I know we need to go to work. Thank you for taking care of me. I hope I can return the favor sometime."

"You do, every time you smile at me."

"That is easy to do" she answered back. Moving closer to him she kissed him gently on the lips. "I'm going to brush my teeth. Can I expect eggs benedict when I come back?"

"Of course, in the shape of a pumpernickel bagel."

Alex got the butter and cream cheese and put them on the small counter in his kitchen. Bagels were placed in the toaster oven ready to start as soon as he heard the bathroom door open. He only had one chair in the kitchen so set up two place settings on the coffee table in the living room. He heard the bathroom door open and 'started' breakfast.

He took two beakers of coffee to the living room.

"Here is your coffee, just the way you like it… with a little cream and no sugar. Bagels will be ready any minute."

"I'm not used to being treated this way. Am I supposed to leave a tip?

"Only if the service is good."

"I don't have enough money in my bank account to cover that."

Alex brought in a tray of bagels, butter and cream cheese and put it on the coffee table as he sat down next to Leslie.

"This is all I have. I wasn't expecting a guest for breakfast."

This is more than enough…I usually only have a cup of coffee.

"How are you doing? Yesterday was a big day for you."

"I don't think I have totally comprehended what is happening. It is all so surreal."

"It is a lot for you to take in and try to wrap your mind around. Let's take it one step at a time."

"I just wish I could remember more about the experience ten years ago. I was so groggy in the hospital that everything is a fog. I just accepted everything I was told. I thought it was all over and behind me. Now this."

"Maybe memories will start coming back now that there is a reason."

"I can't believe my father knows anything more. We never had secrets."

"He only did what he had to do to protect you. It had probably been a big weight on him all these years that you don't know what happened. Especially if Sara is alive and living somewhere."

"Every time I hear her name, it makes it so real."

"She may be real and out there, Leslie."

"That is the part that is hard to believe…that she may be out there somewhere. If so, does she know about me?"

Leslie looked straight ahead as if in another world. A look of sadness came across her face. Alex just watched her, deep in thoughts of his own. Thoughts of how he could help her and take care of her.

"Leslie, it is getting late. We need to be at work in ninety minutes. We better get ready. I'll let you shower first while I clean up from breakfast."

She turned toward him, still in thought.

"Oh yes, we should." Taking the last sip of her coffee the expression on her faced changed to happiness. "I'd ask you to join me in the shower...to save water of course...but then we would be really late to work."

With that she got up and headed to the bathroom. Alex just stood there and watched her, his coffee still in his hand. Taking a sip of his coffee he picked up the plates and headed to the kitchen. He then called the police number on the card and told them that the two of them would be leaving to go to work in about forty-five minutes.

Thirty minutes later Leslie enter the living room, dressed in a dark green pants suit, her hair in place and makeup flawless.

"Your turn. Want me to come scrub your back?"

"Yes... but not enough time" Alex responded with a wink as he headed to the bedroom. "I'll take a raincheck."

'You got it."

Twenty minutes later he entered the living room dressed in business casual...light blue long sleeve shirt and black slacks, his hair still a little wet. He ran his fingers through his hair to push it into place.

"Let's go" he said as he picked up his keys and backpack by the door. He held the door for Leslie, and she headed to the elevator as he locked the door.

The doorman welcomed them with a cheery 'good morning' as he held the front door open for them. As they descended the front steps Alex saw the two unmarked cars in the 'no parking' zone. The driver and passenger seat door opened, and two men got out. Alex recognized the driver. It was the policeman assigned to 'protect' him. The other man must have been the policeman assigned to Leslie.

"Where are you going sir" the policeman asked Alex

"We are on our way to work."

"Allow us to take you there."

"We both work at the same place, so we only need one car."

The policeman held the back door open and they got in. As he moved to the driver side, the other policeman got in his car and left. Alex gave the policeman the address and sat back to enjoy the ride.

The policeman turned around and gave each of them another card with a telephone number on it. When you get ready to leave work give us a call at the number on the card and we will pick you up and take you to where you need to go. Since tomorrow is Saturday you will need to call us before your leave your apartment so we can follow you. Understand?"

"Yes sir. Thank you. But you gave me a card yesterday."

"Doesn't hurt to have a backup."

With that the police turned around, started the car, and headed toward midtown.

"It takes me twenty-five minutes door to door to get to the office. Let's see how long this takes."

"Traffic is always heavy in midtown" the policeman responded. "You would get there faster by subway. But this way is safer."

Thirty minutes later they pulled up in front of the office building on Park Avenue.

"Remember to call that number before you leave the office so we can be here. If you leave the office anytime during day, please call us first and let us know."

"Yes sir."

Alex and Leslie entered the office, the officer escorting them until they were in the lobby.

"I could travel like that every day, rather than being shoved into the overcrowded subways."

"Don't get used to it" Leslie responded.

They went through the security gates and then to separate elevators to get to their respective work areas.

"I'll meet you for lunch...same place, same time" Alex said as Leslie got onto the private elevator. The door closed and she was gone.

I hope she is okay being alone Alex thought as he waited for his elevator to arrive.

Alex entered his office and settled in.

"Happy Friday, Dr. Gregory."

Alex looked up to see Lindsey standing in the doorway.

"Happy Friday to you too. How is the day looking?"

"Normal Friday for me...not sure what that means for you. I'm going to get some coffee. Want me to get you some?"

"Thank you. That would be very nice. Here is my cup." Alex got up and handed her his cup.

"Looks like it needs a good cleaning. I'll do that before I fill it" Lindsey replied as she turned and left the office.

"If you do that you will remove all the flavor" Alex responded with a smile. "Thanks Lindsey."

Just then another figure appeared in the door.

"Andrea Cushman. We haven't met yet" she said as she walked over to Alex, hand extended. She was carrying an arm full of folders that she tried to juggle at the same time.

"Good to meet you. I understand you are my new boss."

"Just temporarily. Gene said nothing but good things about you."

"Thank you."

"Since we are no longer going to promote 57162, we have some new products in the pipe-line I'd like to have you look at the data and give us your opinion of their potential." She put the pile of folders on the corner of his desk.

"I'll start looking at it right away. It will be good to have a project again."

With that Andrea turned and left the room without saying another word.

Alex picked up the first folder and opened it. Lindsey quietly walked to his desk and put down the coffee cup and left without a word.

Alex spent the rest of the morning looked at the data. He looked at his watched and saw that it was 11:45…time for lunch. Just then the phone rang.

"Dr. Gregory here."

"Hello Dr. Gregory. This is Lisa Fisher from the District Attorney's office. I just wanted to let you know that we have received confirmation that Mr. Tony Neuman is no long in the New York area and therefore you are no longer in any danger from him. As a result, there is no need for us to provide you with twenty-four protection. If anything changes, we will let you know. We have also contacted Ms. Hudson and Ms. Sherwood and provided them with the same information. As we get closer to the actual trial, we will contact you as a witness to help you with your statements to the court. Again, thank you for your time and go on as if nothing ever happened. Are there any questions?"

"Not right now but I'm sure there will be some later. I was just getting used to the chauffer" Alex answered back. There was no response on the other end.

"Then good-day Dr. Gregory. We will be in contact soon." With that the line went dead.

That was short and dull Alex thought as he left his office and headed to the cafeteria. As he entered the cafeteria, he saw Leslie siting at a table anxiously staring at the door waiting for him.

"You didn't have to wait for me" he said as he sat down. She looked so beautiful He wanted to take her in his arms and kiss her, but as always…not the time and place.

"I have done nothing but think about Sara all morning."

Alex could see the joy in her face when she said the name but at the same time concern, and anxiety.

"Is something bothering you?"

"I have to find out where she is and if she is okay. I remembered this morning that I think I have the name of the couple who were going to adopt her written down someplace. If I do, maybe that is a starting point. What do you think?"

"Sounds like the start of a plan. But Leslie, let's not get too excited and get our hopes up. There is possibility for disappointment."

"I know…but I have to do something. and this is the best I can think of. What if she really is in trouble and needs me?"

"Let's see if you can find a name and we will start from there. Right now, I'm hungry. Let's eat."

Alex was concerned about Leslie. As he looked at her, he could see she was in deep thought. He wanted to help her find the truth but didn't want her to be hurt. How could either one of them eat with thoughts going through their heads, her about her missing child and him about the upcoming trial and the status of Sara.

Is she alive? Is she well? Is she happy? Where is she? What about his testimony?

Thought after thought went throw his head. When will it all be over? Then his thoughts turned to the phone call he got from the district attorney's office.

Tony escaped. Are they safe from him? Is he really in Canada?

Chapter 16

*U*ptown in Harlem in a walk-up brownstone, Tony Neuman sat at the kitchen table by a window of a second-floor apartment, an apartment rented by a fellow 'thug' friend of his. A place for him to hide for a while. With a cold beer in his hand he sat watching the people on the street below going about their everyday routine. He had to smile to himself as he pressed the bottle to his lips. He knew it was too early in the morning to start drinking, but there was a need to celebrate his accomplishments over the past weeks, and this was his way of saying "good job".

If the people below only knew who was watching them. But then again, he was probably not the only fugitive hiding away uptown. The police were probably not looking for him anymore since they think he is in Canada. Let the Canadians do the looking for him. His plan seems to be working.

His last two weeks have been full, most of it hiding from the police once he escaped from jail. But with each passing day he was convinced that he wouldn't be found before he headed to south American, to a country with no extradition agreement with the United States.

After two days in county jail. he realized that jail is a place he did not want to spend any portion of his remaining life. He therefore turned all his attention from surviving in jail to figuring out a way to get out and disappear. His carefully orchestrated plan seems to have worked. Just a few more tasks to be completed before he headed to someplace in South America, living on the money he had hidden in an offshore account. Money he had received as a 'consultant' for Sterling Chemicals. He was sure there was no written job description for his consulting.

Tony Gianti, Senior Vice President at Sterling, didn't want the facts of the new product to come out. He wanted his big bonus and plush job at the company. He had hired Tony Neuman to help him cover up the secret, by eliminating anyone who got close to the product's secrets. Tony's latest assignment was to 'eliminate' Alex Gregory. The method of 'elimination' was up to him provided there was no link back to the company.

Alex had unearthed company documents that proved that the new product Sterling was about to market was very detrimental to the environment. In fact, it was so bad that it could eliminate humanity over several generations. As a result of his findings, Alex started to question the death of two former employees at Sterling who were also concerned about this product and who were getting too close to the truth.

Alex Gregory was getting too close to the truth and he was next on the list. Tony Neuman had suggested a plan to get rid of both Alex and his girlfriend. His plan was simple. Alex and Leslie were schedule to go on a business trip to West Virginia where Sterling had their manufacturing plants. There are lots of places for two people to just disappear in that state. Mountains and gullies for a car to accidently miss a turn and plunge over a cliff. Tony Gianti had suggested the trip to Alex's boss, convincing him it would in his best interest to understand how the company works. Leslie was to also schedule to visit the plant as well. Since she worked for the Senior Vice President of manufacturing, he convinced her boss that she should meet the people responsible for the products at the West Virginia plant. Everything was arranged.

But right before the two of them were to travel to West Virginia on company business, they disappeared. Rumors circulated around the company that they had died in an automobile accident. A car Alex had rented was found in the Hudson River. Shortly after that Tony was arrested. Then a week later Alex and Leslie mysteriously showed up at work. Alex had provided the police with information about 'accidents' at the company before he had a chance to create Alex's accident.

Alex was responsible for Tony Neuman's arrest. He pounded his fist on the table as he thought of Alex. It gave him pleasure thinking that Alex would disappear again, and he would be part of it. And this would be for real.

He thought back to the day he was arrested. He was leaving his rented apartment in Long Island when three police cars pulled up and six policemen jumped out with guns. Before he knew it, his hands were handcuffed behind his back and he was in the backseat of a police car heading to jail.

He thought he could handle prison, but it was far worse than he had imagined. It was the loneliness that got to him. There he sat hour after hour in a small cell, with no one to talk to and no place to go. Someone else had control of his every move...when he got up, when he showered, when he ate, command after command...all day long. After a couple of days, he decided this life was not for him and he had to find a way to get out. As he sat there hour after hour a plan was forming in his mind.

He had to find someone on the outside to help him with. He had a person in mind...Nick. Nick owed him big time. The plan was simple. Nick would park outside the courthouse and watch the comings and goings of the prisoners from prison to the courthouse, recording the proceeds in great detail...was there certain time of day prisoners were transferred, were they in handcuffs, how were they dressed, how many guards, how long was the walk from transport to the courthouse door. Tony needed to know every detail about how prisoners were transported to the courthouse.

Tony and Nick never met or called each other while they planned for his escape. There had to be no contact between them so nothing could be traced back to either of them. Nick got information to Tony through an inmate housed in the same cell block.

The plan was simple...a simple plan has less chances of anything going wrong. The day arrived for Tony to be taken to the courthouse. He was dressed in street clothes and no handcuffs. Just two guards assigned to him.

As the transport van approached the back of the courthouse, Tony looked around for Nick. There he was. Sitting in a black SUV about 200 feet away, the side door slowly opening as the prison van slowed down. Nick's body tensed, ready for the run.

Suddenly there was an explosion half a block away, set up by Nick and triggered by his phone. The guards turned to see what was happening, loosening their grip of Tony's arm for a slip second. It was enough time for him to pull away and sprint off toward the open door of the SUV. He had a good start on the police, and they couldn't keep up with him. He dove into the back seat grabbing the seat belt and holding on as Nick sped off, the door still open.

Once they got around the corner out of sight of the courthouse, Nick slowed, and Tony jumped out, ducking into the lobby of the closest building. Nick then continued down the street. As Tony stood in the lobby of the building two police cars raced by with sirens on.

"Good Luck Boys."

From that day on he has been watching over his shoulder, wherever he went. At first it dominated his every move. Now, enough time had passed that he felt safe. Nick had ditched the untraceable SUV. Stage one of this plan was complete.

Two days ago, he initiated the second part of his plan. He needed to give some false clues to the police so everyone would believe he had fled the country. Again, he turned to Nick. Nick drove up to the Canadian border. When no one was looking, he carefully placed an opened envelope that would be found by the border guards with Tony's name and address on it. He made it look like the envelope had fallen out of the car as it was heading into Canada. It was an envelope that Tony brought with him from the jail that he had received while incarcerated. That way it had the date and jail stamp on it. While he was lying on the backseat of the SUV during the escape Tony pulled the envelope out of his pants and left it on the floor of the van for Nick to use.

Tony had heard on the news that he had escaped, and the police believe that he fled the country into Canada. Part two of his planned completed. Now for the final step of his plan...get rid of Alex Gregory.

Chapter 17

*A*lex woke up to the smell of coffee. Leslie was not in bed next to him. Since it was Saturday, he was hoping they would sleep in but didn't look like that would happen. He slowly got out of bed, put on a pair of running shorts and t-shirt, ran his fingers through his hair and headed to the living room. Leslie was sitting there alone, a cup of coffee in her hands.

"I hope I didn't wake you. I had to search your kitchen to find the coffee."

"That didn't take long I'm sure. My kitchen is only big enough for one person at a time. Not many places to hide coffee" he said as he leaned over and kissed Leslie on the cheek. "I hope there is some left for me."

"I made a full pot."

Alex headed to the kitchen, filled his cup…best way to start a day. He headed back to the living room, cup in hand and sat down next to Leslie.

"I'm glad it is Saturday. We can have a leisurely morning. I usually get up early and head to the gym, but it was so nice to sleep in a little today. I know you didn't have a peaceful night. You tossed and turned all night again. But that was expected with what you went through yesterday. How are you doing?"

I'm sorry if I kept you awake but I did have a fitful night. Images just kept going through my head. I thought all of this was behind me and now someone opened all the feelings again with that note. What is going on Alex?"

"I don't know Leslie. But we will find the answer and get through this together. Right now, I need this delicious coffee you made."

"You always know what to say. You are a real charmer."

"That's me… charm from head to toe…for the right person."

Silence.

"I got up early this morning and have been sitting here thinking about what has happened. I'm convinced that Sara is alive somewhere close by and someone thinks she needs me. The only people who could have her are the couple that were going to adopt her."

"That is a possibility."

"My father arranged for them to take the baby and then came up with the story that Sara died to spare me" Leslie continued as if not hearing Alex.

Alex just sat their listening.

"Alex, we have to find them" she said turning and looking directly at him, determination in her voice.

"But we don't know who they are. And it might not be a good idea to ask your dad. He has kept this secret for a long time to protect you. Are you sure you want to go down that route?"

"I have to think of Sara first and my father second. What if Sara is in trouble and really needs me? I can't let that happen. I need to go back to Brooklyn, Alex, and see if I can find the name of the adoptive parents. I'm sure I wrote it down someplace. I must do this Alex… I have to find the end to this story, whatever it is."

"I just have a hard time believing that the people who were going to adopt her would harm her. Your father is too thorough to let someone get his granddaughter who might harm here."

"That is why is hard for me to believe that they have Sara and would harm her. But we need to start someplace. Maybe they know something."

"You're right. Let's finish our coffee, go have some breakfast and head back to your place and see if you can find the paper with their name on it."

"Let's skip breakfast and just go to my place. We can pick up some bagels at the corner deli. I need to do this now Alex. I hope you understand."

"I understand. Let's get dressed and head to the subway. We can save time if we shower together."

Leslie looked up at him, her lips slightly curved up. "I agree with you" she said as she grabbed his hand and headed to the bathroom.

◆

An hour later they were on the subway heading toward Brooklyn. Neither one said a word...deep in thought. Alex was worried about Leslie. If the child is alive and they find her, how will Leslie react? What would she do then? And if there is no child...how will that affect her. And how will all of this affect him and their relationship. It is a deep hole and he has not idea of what will come out of it?

The train stopped at the Clark Street station in Brooklyn Heights and they exited. It was a short walk to the deli to get bagels and then to Leslie's apartment.

"I must have the name here someplace" Leslie said as they entered her apartment. She immediately went to the desk in the

corner and started going through the drawers. She was a woman on a mission. Alex went to the kitchen, made a pot of coffee, and put the bagels in the toaster. He put the toasted bagels on a tray, the coffee pot and cups and returned to the living room. "Breakfast" he yelled.

Leslie appeared from the bedroom with a wooden box in her hand. She sat down next to Alex and opened the box. There was a book on top that she pulled out and put on the sofa next to her. She continued going through the box pulling out and reading one piece of paper after another. Closing the box, she put it on the table in front of her and picked up a bagel. Alex poured her a cup of coffee.

"I thought for sure that I had written the name down on a piece of paper and put it in that box" she said taking a bite from the bagel. "Thanks for the coffee" she added, leaning over and giving Alex a kiss on the cheek then sitting back deep in thought.

All Alex could do was to sit back and let her think. This was their mission, but she had to take the lead. He would be there when she needed him.

"What's this?" Alex asked picking up the book that Leslie had put on the sofa between them as she went through the box paper.

"It is my diary that I kept while in high school."

"You kept a diary? Any racy things I should know about?"

"I stopped writing in there once I graduated. I had a very dull teen period so am sure there is nothing of interest in there. Just girly stuff."

"List of old boyfriends? Maybe I need to check it out."

"Nothing you would be interested in."

"Are you sure?"

"Go ahead. In fact, read it out loud to me so we can both have a good laugh."

Alex picked up the book and opened to the first page. "Your first entry. It says 'I got this book last week from my daddy for my birthday. Today, Mike smiled at me in math class and I got goose bumps.' My oh my, I have competition."

"I think I was twelve when I wrote that. But he did have a cute smile."

Alex quickly paged through the diary, stopping now and then to read a passage out loud. Leslie just sat there and smiled and once during a rather passionate message she blushed. Suddenly Alex stopped paging through the diary and was reading a page to himself. He looked up at Leslie.

"Here are your notes about your attack. I don't think I should read them…they are your private thoughts" he said handing the diary to Leslie.

Leslie took the book and starting reading. Her face went from joy to anger and sadness. Alex just sat and watched as she read page after page. Suddenly she stopped and looked at Alex.

"Kirk and Mary Ellen Thompson, New Haven, Connecticut" she said softy and then looked at Alex, pointing to the writing on the page. "This is the couple who were going to adopt Sara. Right here in my diary. They must have Sara. Right Alex?"

"Let's not jump to conclusions. It has been ten years. A lot of time has passed by."

"But this is a start. We need to check it out. Let's go there Alex. We can drive up today. Please? I have to know."

"Not so fast. First, let's Google them and see if they are listed in New Haven."

Alex took out his phone and started searching on this phone trough several search engines and found the name Kirk and Mary Ellen Thompson listed in New Haven. But there was no address or phone number provided.

"Let's rent a car now and drive up. I can't just sit around here and worry. I must do something."

"Hold on, we can't just barge in one them asking questions. We don't know anything about them or the situation. Remember, if Sara is with them, they have a legal right."

"I have to know if Sara is okay. I don't want to upset her, but the red headed woman says she needs me. I need to find out Alex. Please?"

"But…" Alex started.

"If you don't want to do anything I'll go alone. There is car rental place close by."

"Okay. You win. But we have to be logical about this and respect their privacy."

"Thank you, Alex."

"It is a nice day, and the drive will be a pleasant one. I know this is an argument I could never win."

"You are right about that" Leslie said, giving Alex a kiss on the cheek. She picked up the cups and took them into the kitchen.

"We can also stop in and see your parents and see if they received any message." Alex yelled to Leslie in the kitchen.

"Let's not stop by. I'm not ready to confront them yet."

"Okay. It is only a two-hour drive. It will be good to get out of the city and I don't want you going there alone. It could be dangerous. "

"Dangerous? How could this be dangerous? We are talking about my daughter."

Pause…

"It just dawned on me, that is the first time I called her 'my daughter'. Please Alex, let's go now."

Alex couldn't bare the look of disappointment on Leslie's face if they didn't' check this out. "Yes, this could be dangerous. We know nothing about these people. We can't just rush in."

"How could this be dangerous? My father researched the couple thoroughly."

"That was ten years ago. We have no idea what has happened the last ten years. Does Sara know she was adopted? You can't just rush in and upset a family and upset her."

Leslie stood there staring at Alex.

"How are you going to feel if Sara is happy, but doesn't know she was adopted? How is that going to affect you?"

"I can't worry about me. I must make sure Sara is all right. Wow, I'm sounding like a mother."

"You are a mother."

Silence.

"Please Alex. I have to know."

"How can I resist when you look at me that way."

"Is it working?"

"Okay, but you are in no condition to do this on your own. You need to let me run the show. You are too emotionally involved. Promise me you will do what I suggest, or at least consider it?"

"Of course," is all she said as they headed toward the door, Alex still standing in the middle of the room.

"Of course," he said to himself. "Here we go."

Chapter 18

*A*s Leslie was locking her door Mrs. Sester came out of her apartment.

"Good morning Leslie" she said as she shut her door. "You are up early today. This is the weekend. I thought all young people sleep in" she said giving a wicked smile at Alex.

'It was such a nice day, we thought we would rent a car and drive to New Haven to visit my parents" she lied.

"That sounds like a wonderful way to spend the day."

"Where are you heading so early?" Leslie asked.

"I'm just going down to the corner deli and get bagel and cup of coffee. Something I do every weekend. Gets me up and out of the apartment."

They reached the bottom of the stairs and left the building together. The three of them walked to the corner together enjoying each other's company. Mrs. Sester turned right and crossed the street once they reached to corner.

"Have a good time" Mrs. Sester said as she headed to the deli.

"You too, Mrs. Sester. Enjoy your bagel" Alex responded with a short wave.

They continued to walk straight ahead toward the car rental place a few blocks away. They rented a car for the day and they were on their way to New Haven. Checking the GPS on the car it would be an easy trip. They left Brooklyn at 10:30 and were on the outskirts of New Haven by 12:30. There was little conversation along the way. Alex tried to engage in conversation, but Leslie was deep in thought of her own.

"We need to discuss how to approach this, Leslie. Let's stop for lunch and come up with some ideas."

"Okay" is all that Leslie said.

Alex pulled off the expressway and pulled into the parking lot of a diner. The diner was right out of the fifties. Stainless steel on the outside with large picture windows. As they walked in, they felt like they had entered a different era. There where banquette booths along that wall of red vinyl seats with chrome tables. The top of the table was white Formica that had grey streaks through it. The floor was a checkerboard of vinyl tiles. Along one wall was a counter with stools with the same red vinyl seats, rimmed with chrome. The stools were attached to the floor and the seats swiveled for easy sitting. Behind the counter were two malt machines in line green on a black counter. In one corner of the diner was a jukebox. On the wall was a wall-mounted pay phone. Above it was a chrome wall clock. Fluorescent lights hung from the ceiling.

They were escorted to a booth and given menus.

"I don't know about you, but I'm going to have a malt" Alex said breaking the silence. "Rich Chocolate."

"That sounds good, but I think I will have an egg crème, and a garden salad" Leslie stated looking at her menu.

"This is a fifties diner so I'm going to eat like the fifties...a cheeseburger with fries for me."

A waitress approached the table to take their order. She was wearing a red dress with white collar and white sleeves. A white half apron with a black belt was tied over the dress. A matching hat was atop her head.

"May I take your order?"

Alex gave her their orders and she left without a word.

"I expect Elvis to walk in any moment" Alex said trying to start a conversation. "I should also have greased my hair into a ducktail."

"You would look funny with a ducktail haircut."

"But I'd blend in with this diner."

"So, what do we do now Alex?"

"Too bad everyone today uses cell phones. In the past you could go to a phone book and look up the address of a person. There was usually a phone book at every phone booth" Alex responded pointing to the phone on the wall. "I'll have to assume that the wall phone is for display purposes only."

Alex took out his cell phone. "Let me do a search on White Pages and got an address for the Thompsons."

Alex punched several keys then started scrolling down the screen of his phone. "Apparently they are still in New Haven. Here is a listing for Kirk Thompson on Saint Ronan Street."

"Let's go!"

"Don't you think we should eat our lunch first?"

"I guess that would be a good idea."

Alex tried to keep a conversation going away from their current adventure, but Leslie wasn't listening. So eventually he just stopped talking and concentrating on eating. He noticed that she played with her food more than she ate, constantly watching him eat, as if wishing he would eat faster.

"I'm finished" she said as she saw Alex put the last French fry in his mouth, her salad only half eaten.

Alex waved for the waitress and once they got the check Leslie was out of the booth heading to the door. Alex left the tip on the table, moved to the cashier, paid the bill, and met Leslie who was waiting outside.

"Here's the plan, Leslie" Alex started as they got into the car and before he started the engine. "We will find the house, drive by it and then drive around the neighborhood to get a feeling of the area. That is as far as I have planned. What do you have in mind?"

"I have no idea. Right now, I'm just a bunch of emotions and all kinds of thoughts are going through my head. I'm no good at this."

Alex thought for a while.

"How about this. If everything goes okay, I'll go up to the door and you stay in the car. I'll make up some excuse why I am there and find out if there are any children in the home. If there is a young girl of 10 years of age, I'll explain why I am there. Afterall, if Sara is part of the family she is legally adopted, and we have no say in her future. We are just there to make sure she is okay. Then it will be up to the mother to decide if she will let you meet Sara. What do you think about that? Remember, Sara is legally theirs. We must go by their wishes."

After a moment of silence, Leslie responded.

"You are right. We are here just to make sure that she is all right. I did agree to give her up for adoption and I will abide by that. I just want to make sure that she is okay and not in any danger. I would like to see her and meet her, however. But I know that must be the decision of her mother, not me. I don't want to add any stress to Sara's life. She may not know that she is even adopted."

"So, we have a plan" Alex responded, as he started the car and left the parking lot of the diner.

They drove in silence, following the directions of the GPS.

"Turn left at the next corner onto Saint Ronan Street. Go two tenths of a mile to your destination on the left side of the street" the voice came from the GPS system.

Alex turned left and they slowly drove down the street. Leslie sat forward looking out the front window at every house on the street.

"There it is!" she said pointing to a blue house in the middle of the block.

Alex slowed down more. A blue Victorian Gabled house. Both Leslie and Alex looked at the house as the car moved past it.

"Did you see that? Leslie said excitedly.

"See what?"

"There was a kid's bicycle laying on the front lawn. There must be a child in that home."

Alex continued down the street to the corner and continued for a few blocks and then circled back on the next street over. It was a well-established neighborhood with large older homes with manicured lawns and mature trees. The lots were large, and there were multiple cars in most driveways.

Alex turned back on to Saint Ronan Street and parked across the street from the blue house. He turned to Leslie. She just sat there; eyes glued to the blue house.

"Are you okay?" he asked as he grabbed her hand. She was clutching her fists. "Everything will be fine. I am going to go up to the house now as we discussed. You stay in the car."

Leslie nodded.

Alex let loose of Leslie hand, got out of the car, and headed toward the house. He looked back to see if Leslie was okay. She had moved to the driver's seat and opened the window, her face just staring at the house. He could see that she was biting her lower lip in anticipation…a habit that she had without knowing she was doing it. It was usually an enduring trait, but not today. Alex gave her a slight wave and moved to the front entrance of the house. She gave no response back, eyes glued to the front door of the house,

Alex rang the doorbell. He turned again to see Leslie starring at him from the car. The front door opened, and a woman was standing there.

"I'm sorry to bother you, but I'm conducting a survey for a research project at Yale and wonder if you would answer a few questions for me."

"Thank you but I'm not interested in being part of any survey."

A car door slammed, and they both looked toward the street at the same time. Leslie was walking across the street toward the house at a fast pace.

The woman watched for a few seconds, stepped outside a few steps, and exclaimed "Oh, my God...Leslie?"

Chapter 19

"*H*ello, Mrs. Thompson" Leslie said as she walked up the front sidewalk, her eyes staring at Mrs. Thompson face.

Mary Ellen walked to Leslie and put her arms around her. Leslie did not return the hug.

"It is so good to see you again" Mary Ellen said.

"Mom, can I have a juice?' came from a child standing in the door.

Everyone turned to the door. Standing there was a boy about 10 years of age.

"Of course, you can. Get one from the refrigerator. Come here Mikey, I want you to meet someone. This is a good friend of mine, Leslie Sherwood. She lives in New York City."

"Hi" Mikey responded.

Leslie just stood there looking at the children. Slowly she said "Hi Mikey. It is good to meet you."

With that the child disappeared back into the house, probably on his way to the kitchen to get his juice.

"Are you two together?" Mary Ellen asked looking at Alex.

"Yes, we are" Alex responded.

Come in both of you" Mary Ellen said motioning the two of them into the house.

Alex just stood there, not knowing what to do, his eyes on Leslie. He could not read her face.

Leslie followed Mary Ellen into the house. They moved into the living room, Alex and Leslie sitting on a sofa with Mary Ellen sitting in a chair across from them. The room was nicely done that gave a feeling of home. The back of the living room was all windows overlooking a large fenced-in backyard with a swing set in one corner. Banging noises came from below them. Someone must be in the basement.

"I'm sorry, I don't know your name" Mary Ellen said looking at Alex.

"I'm sorry. I'm Alex Gregory, a friend of Leslie's. We drove up together. I'm sorry about the Yale survey thing. It was a crude way to try to determine if you had a child."

"I'm sorry, I don't understand" Mary Ellen said.

Alex looked at Leslie to see if she wanted to explain. When she didn't say anything, he explained why they were they. How they received a note that Sara needed Leslie when everyone thought that she had died at birth. How they found the Thompson's address and had to come up to see if by chance they had the child.

Mary Ellen sat there and listened to every word, her eyes never leaving Alex's face. Once Alex stopped talking, she turned toward Leslie. She got up from the chair and moved over to the sofa and grabbed Leslie's hand.

"I'm so sorry Leslie. What you must have gone through all these years."

"What do you mean?" Leslie asked, looking very serious at Mary Ellen face.

Mary Ellen turned to Alex, looking for a sign that she should continue.

"Do you know something?" Alex asked.

"Apparently, you have been misinformed all these years. I'm so sorry."

Alex got up from the sofa and moved to the chair across from the sofa so he could see Leslie and Mary Ellen directly. Mary Ellen just sat there looking at Leslie, still holding her hand.

"Then you don't know. You were never told. I'm so sorry. Wait a second, let me get my husband. He is in the basement."

Mary Ellen got up and headed to kitchen. They heard footsteps going down the stairs, then some quiet talking and two sets of footsteps coming up the stairs.

"Leslie and Alex, this is my husband Kirk. I explained to him why you are here."

Alex stood as they entered the room. Kirk extended his hand to Alex. "I'm glad to meet you both. I wish it could be under different circumstances."

"Thank you for talking to us" Alex responded.

Kirk sat down in the other chair opposite Leslie. Mary Ellen returned to the sofa. Alex sat back down and turned to Mr. Thompson.

"We are confused Mr. Thompson. I don't understand. What do you mean 'under different circumstances'?" Can you tell us what happened in the hospital? Did Sara die?" Alex asked.

Silence.

"Let us tell you what we know" Kirk said looking at both Alex and Leslie. Then to his wife. "Go ahead Mary Ellen."

"Ten years ago, my husband and I decided we needed to adopt. We had tried for years to become pregnant, but we couldn't. It was due to a medical imbalance with my hormones. We started looking at adoption agencies and filling out one form after the other. Nothing happened. Then one day a member of our church told us she knew of a family who was looking for someone to adopt a baby soon to be born. This woman was the executive secretary to a President of a bank. That was your father."

Leslie never knew how her father found the Thompsons. Now she did. She just remembered them showing up at the hospital one day and her father introducing them to her.

"We were so happy that we found you. We fell in love with you and your family the moment we met you. Your family told us your story. I'm felt so sorry for you Leslie, yet so close."

"But I gave birth to a baby girl, and you have a son."

"I guess that would be confusing. No, once we knew we would not get your baby, we continued with the adoption process and eventually got Mikey. He is the joy of our life."

"So, Sara did die in the hospital that night" Alex said.

Mary Ellen turned to Alex and then back to Leslie.

"We got a call from your father that you gave birth to a baby girl at about 11:00 pm December 9th. That date has been etched in my brain all these years. We were so excited. I wanted to jump into the car that night and drive to the hospital. But being so late, we decided to wait until morning. We didn't sleep that entire night. We were so excited. We were in the car at 7 A.M the next morning on the way to the hospital."

Leslie continued to look at Mary Ellen, her eyes never leaving her face. Mary Ellen continued holding her hand, her eyes never leaving Leslie face. Leslie made no indication that she felt Mary Ellen's hand.

"We arrived at the hospital and headed to your room. There were two policemen standing outside your room and wouldn't let us in" Kirk stated.

"Police?" Leslie said turning to Kirk.

"Yes, police. Your father never told you?" Kirk asked.

"No. He didn't say anything."

Mary Ellen looked at Alex and then at Leslie, not knowing what to say.

"Then you don't know what happened." Mary Ellen said.

"Know what?" Alex asked.

"I'm not sure it is my place to tell you."

"If you know something, you have to tell me. I must know what happened." Leslie said.

Silence…

Mary Ellen looked at her husband and then back to Leslie.

Kirk gave her a nod to go ahead.

"Your baby was kidnapped from the hospital that night."

Silence.

"Kidnapped?" is all Leslie could say, looking at Mary Ellen, then over to Alex and back to Mary Ellen.

"Your father came out of the room and told us. He said that the baby was in the nursery and that sometime during the night it was taken. The night nurse left the station for a few minutes and when she returned the baby was gone."

"Kidnapped" is all Leslie said in a soft voice staring intently at Mary Ellen.

"The police were called" Mary Ellen continued. They questioned all the nurses and doctors in the hospital and ruled them all out. The police also questioned us for days after. I'm so sorry Leslie."

"I never knew" Leslie said.

"Your father told us we were never to tell you what happened and that he was going to tell you that the baby had died. He also asked us never to contact you again."

"That is why I never heard from you again" Leslie stated.

"I'm so sorry Leslie. What you must have gone through."

"Then Sara is alive" Leslie said softly.

Leslie looked toward Alex. Tears were flowing down her cheek. Mary Ellen moved from the sofa and Alex came over and sat next to

Leslie, taking her in his arms holding her tightly. Several minutes passed and then Leslie pulled away from Alex, looking into his eyes.

"My baby is alive and out there someplace. We need to find her Alex. She needs me."

"We will find her. She needs us both" Alex said.

Leslie turned toward Mary Ellen. "Thank you so much for telling me the truth. We are so sorry to bother you. But I'm glad we did. We will leave now. Again, we are sorry to bother you."

"So, the baby's name is Sara. That is very pretty name" Mary Ellen added. I hope she is fine and happy and that you get a chance to meet her. You would be a great mother."

"Thank you" Leslie responded.

"I hope you find her" Kirk added.

"I'm sorry that we bothered you, but now I am glad that we did stop by" Leslie repeated. "I just had to know."

"It was no bother. You have always been in our thoughts. We have wondered what happened to you through the years but felt we needed to obey your father's wishes. Now that you know the truth, please keep in touch. Please let us know when you find Sara."

"Thank you, I will."

"We better go. Thank you again for your time and information" Alex said as he got up from the sofa and headed to the door.

At the door Leslie turned to Mary Ellen and gave her a hug. "Thank you so much."

"You're welcome. Please keep in touch and let us know how you are doing."

"I will. Again, thank you both."

Leslie turned and joined Alex on the front sidewalk and headed back to the car. As they pull away from the curb they looked back at the blue house. Mary Ellen was still standing in the doorway, with her arm around her son who had joined her. Kirk's arms were around his wife.

As they drove down the street Leslie turned to Alex. "Thank you." She leaned over and kissed him on the cheek. He in return removed his hand from the steering wheel and grabbed Leslie's hand.

"Sara is alive, and we will find her" he said.

"Yes, we will."

As they left the neighborhood Leslie turned back to Alex.

"Let's go talk to my father and see if he can add to the story."

"Are you sure you want to let him know that you know what happened?"

"Yes. He may be able to add more."

"Ok, let's go" Alex responded.

Chapter 20

*T*hey pulled into the driveway at Leslie's childhood home. Her parents still lived in the house where she was reared, less than fifteen miles for the Thompsons. Leslie had the car door open before the car was completely stopped. Alex joined her at the front door and stepped in front of her before she entered the house.

"Leslie, your father has kept this secret for ten years now. You can't just march in and accuse him of hiding this secret. You know he has suffered all these years. We aren't even sure if your mother knows what happened. He might have kept it a secret from her too. We need to consider their feelings. Again, I want to suggest that you let me take the lead on this. You are too emotional right now."

Leslie just stared at him, her face going from anger to understanding.

"You are right. I need to put my anger aside. He did what he thought was best. But he needs to know that we know, and we now deserve the truth."

"I agree with you, but we need to approach the topic in a caring way, not angry. Will you agree to let me handle it? At least get the topic started?"

"Okay, as I said before, you are much more diplomatic than I am" she said as she leaned in and gave him a kiss on the cheek.

"You are diplomatic too…just not on this topic" he said returning the kiss.

Alex turned and rang the doorbell.

"No need to ring the bell. This is my home" Leslie said opening the door. As they entered, they saw her mom heading toward the door.

"Leslie, how good to see you. Did I forget that you were going to visit today? Is everything okay?"

"No mom, it was a last-minute decision we made this morning."

Alex saw a look of curiosity in Mrs. Thompson's face.

"No, everything is fine. It was just a nice day and we decided to rent a car and get out of the city. Somehow, we ended up here."

"Hi Alex. Come in both of you. Let me call your dad. He is in the back mowing the lawn. Saturday morning task you know."

The three of them moved to the backyard. Leslie saw her dad pushing the lawn mower at the other end of the yard. Her fist tightened. Alex noticed that and grabbed her hand. Her fist relaxed. Her father turned and noticed them. He waved to them, leaned over, turned off the mower and headed their way.

"Hi Leslie. Hi Alex." He kissed Leslie on the cheek and stretched out his hand to shake hands with Alex. "What brings you two here? Did you know they were stopping by?" he said turning toward his wife?"

"No, it was a surprise to me too. Let's sit and catch up. It is a nice day. Let me get something to eat and drink."

Leslie's mom returned to the kitchen as the three of them sat in the chairs underneath the awing on the patio.

"I am glad you stopped by. We don't see enough of you."

"It was a nice day and we needed to get out of the city and the drive up here was so nice" Alex responded. "I see that some of the trees are already starting to change color for the fall."

Just then Leslie's mother returned with a tray of lemonade and some cookies. "Too late for lunch and too early for dinner, so I thought that cookies would be fine,"

"We came up for a reason" Leslie started looking directly at her father.

"Ah, what Leslie meant to say is that we made this trip to New Haven for a specific reason" Alex remarked interrupting Leslie so he could take control of the conversaton.

"What is that?" Leslie's father asked, reaching forward picking up a glass of lemonade.

"We came up to talk to Kirk and May Ellen Thompson" Leslie stated.

Both Leslie and Alex looked at her dad's face to see the reaction. There was no change. They turned to Leslie's mother and there was a questioning look.

"Why did you want to talk to them?" Leslie's mother asked.

"I think I know" Leslie's dad responded. "They discovered the truth."

"What truth?" Leslie's mother asked.

"The truth about Leslie's baby. Something that happened ten years ago. I've kept the secret from both of you too long."

Silence.

Leslie started to say something, but Alex interrupted. "I'm sorry sir, I was hoping we could approach this subject but not so directly. Something happened yesterday that made it important for us to come see you."

"Time for it to be told. It has eaten away at me every day." Turning to Leslie. "What do you know?"

"What secret?" Leslie's mother asked. "I have no idea what you are talking about."

Before Leslie had a chance to talk, Alex took over the conversation.

"We received an anonymous note that Sara was still alive and needed her mother."

"Who? Leslie's mother responded.

"Sara, my baby" Leslie said.

"But she died in the hospital?"

"That is not true, dear. That is the secret we are talking about. Sara did not die in the hospital" Leslie father said.

Leslie's mother face turned from surprise to not understanding.

"Let me continue" Alex said. "Leslie received a note from a stranger that said, 'Your daughter Sara needs you. Just five words. No name."

"The note was delivered to my neighbor who gave it to me." Leslie added.

"Once we got the note" Alex continued, "we had to find out if it was true. Our first thought was to meet with the potential adopted parents to see if they had the baby and you kept that a secret from Leslie all these years. Leslie had written down their names in her diary. We looked up their address on Google and came up to New Haven this morning to talk to them. We left their home about twenty minutes ago. As you know, they didn't have the baby."

"We know that Leslie" her mother said. "As we told you ten years ago, the baby died."

"That's not true, is it Dad" Leslie stated, looking directly at her father.

"You are right, the baby did not die in the hospital."

"What's going on here?" her mother asked.

"Do you want me to tell her or do you want to tell her?" Leslie responded.

"I'll tell her. I should have done that ten years ago."

"The baby did not die in the hospital. It was kidnapped that night" he said looking at his wife.

All eyes turned to his wife.

"Kidnapped? How? Who?"

"Sometime after the 2 AM shift change the baby was taken from the nursery. The attending nurse stepped away for a moment and when she came back the baby was gone. The next morning when we arrived at the hospital, I was met by the police who told me what had happened. I made a quick decision. Now, I see it was probably a bad one. The truth would have been better. I thought it best to tell everyone that the baby had died. That way Leslie could get on with her life and not wonder what happened to her daughter."

"So, the funeral for Sara was false?" Leslies mother said?

"Yes, I arranged for a mock funeral." Tears appeared in her dad's eyes.

All eyes were on Leslie's father, waiting for more details.

"I did what I thought best under the circumstances. I only wanted to protect my family. I have carried this burden too long; it is good to get it out. I'm sorry baby" he said as he looked at Leslie.

Leslie got up from her chair and moved to her father putting her arms around him. A deep sigh came out of her dad as tears rolled down his checks.

"I understand daddy. You did what you thought best. We can't change the past."

Alex looked at Leslie's face. All the anger had disappeared, only to be replaced with sympathy and understanding.

"Thank you, baby" is all her father could say.

They both turned to look at her mother. She was just sitting there with no expression on her face, but tears running down her check.

"Then I have a granddaughter out there someplace" is all she could say.

"I know mom, and I have a daughter who needs me."

Leslie turned to Alex. He had just been sitting here quietly watching this event unravel. Leslie walked over to him and put her arms around him. "Thank you, Alex" for being there for me she whispered into his ear."

"No place else for me to be" is all he could remark, squeezing Leslie tighter.

Leslie sat down next to Alex. He automatically took her hand and held it. Everyone was quiet, deep in their own thoughts.

Leslie's father looked at Alex and quietly said "Thank you." Alex smiled back.

"Can you tell us what happened after the police arrived?" Alex asked.

"The police met us at the door when we arrived at the hospital the next morning" Leslie's father started. "I motioned the police to be quiet and sent my wife to be with Leslie. No reason for her to be involved. They told me that they received a call at 2:15 AM that Leslie's baby was missing from the hospital. What my wife didn't know is that the police texted my cell phone at 2:20 am. I heard the phone buzz on my bedstand. I called them and they told me what happened. I told them I would be there in the morning and they were not to say anything to my wife or Leslie. I then made up the story that the baby had died during the night. That her lungs were not fully developed, and she went peacefully. It was the hardest thing I ever had to do. The look on your face when I told you is a look that is burned in my mind. I hope I never see it again."

"You've known all these years what happened and didn't tell me" his wife said.

"I was only trying to protect you. I now realize it was a mistake."

"What happened then?" Alex asked.

"When I arrived at the hospital the police were waiting. They took me into a room and told me what they knew. Apparently, someone was hiding in the hospital watching the nursery. When the nurse left, they rushed in and took the baby. There was no indication that they were particularly interested in your baby, Leslie. It looked like a random abduction. There were only three babies in the nursery at that time. Sara was closest to the door. The police issued an ambler alert, but nothing ever came of it. They said they had questioned everyone on the floor, but no one had any additional information. There were no fingerprints on the door of the nursery, so they assumed the kidnapper knew what they were doing, and it was not an abduction by a crazy person."

"Just then the Thompson's showed up. We pulled them aside and told them what happened. They wanted to see you Leslie, to make sure you were okay. I didn't allow that to happen. I didn't want them to give you any information and I asked them to leave and please keep what they know quiet. Not to tell anyone and especially the press what they know. I explained to them that I would tell you and your mom, that the baby died. They agree not to say anything. They were very upset. They wanted me to tell you that they were thinking of you Leslie, and that you were in their prayers. After they left, I went to your room to see how you were doing and to tell you and your mom that the baby had died peacefully during the night."

Alex could see a sign of relief in Mr. Thompson's face as he finished his story. What a burden he had carried all these years. He wondered what he would have done if he was in his shoes.

"So, I have a granddaughter out there someplace" Mrs. Thompson said again.

"What did the police do to try to find the kidnappers?" Alex asked.

"I made sure that the police only worked with me. I didn't want them to upset Leslie or her mother. As I said, they interviewed everyone associated with the nursery. They searched all the security cameras and found nothing suspicious. The cameras in the nursery had been sprayed with black paint as well as the cameras at the side entrances. The police worked on this for months but kept coming up with no leads. Eventually, they just stopped and moved on to other cases. But the case is still open, ten years later. I'm sorry Leslie…I just didn't know what to do."

"That's okay Dad. At least we know that Sara is alive" Leslie stated looking at both her mother and farther. "I have to keep looking."

"Of course, you do, and we want to help in any way we can" her father responded. "What are you feeling Alex, if I may ask"

"I'm with all of you. I'll do whatever I can. We need to find an end to this, wherever it leads us."

"I knew you would say that" Mrs. Thompson said. "Thank you for helping Leslie."

"Do you have any other questions Leslie? I've told you all I know."

"Right now, I can't think of anything else. I'm sure more questions will come up. I thought that part of my life was behind me. When I got that note all my motherly instincts set it. I didn't even know that they even existed."

Leslie's father got up and went into the house. A few minutes later he came back with a file folder and handed it to Alex.

"Here are all the files done by the police about the abduction. Maybe you can find something I've missed. I've gone over these files hundreds of time and nothing new sticks out."

"Thank your sir. Right now, I think Leslie and I need to return to New York. It is a two-hour drive and I want to get back before dark. Afterall, the days are getting shorter."

"I think that best" Leslie added. "A lot has happened over the past 24 hours and I need time to think."

"I wish you would stay the night. I don't want you being alone" her mother added.

"She won't be alone" Alex interjected.

With that, they all got up and headed to the door, a look and feeling of despair and relief on everyone's face.

As they left the front door Leslie turned to her dad. "Thanks for telling me what happened. I'm not upset that you withheld the truth from me all these years." She leaned it and gave her father a kiss on the cheek and whispered in his year. "I'm not sure mom feels the same way."

"I know" her father responded. "But we will get through this. You take care of yourself."

Leslie turned and say good-bye to her mom. She and Alex got into the car, backed out of the driveway, and headed back to New York City.

What a day this has been they both thought to themselves.

Chapter 21

*A*s they left that morning on their way to New Haven, no one noticed the car parked across and down the street from Leslie's apartment. They were all too busy talking and in their own thoughts. The driver watched the old woman cross the street in one direction and go into the deli. Alex and Leslie went straight ahead. Maybe this was the day to start the next phase of his plan. Tony sat there with a smile on his face.

Yes, this is the day.

Tony sat in the car and waited for the older woman to come out of the deli and head back down the street. One thing you learn in prison is patience. He watched her come out of the deli, cross the street and head back to her apartment. When she was about 50 feet from the front of the apartment, he got out of his car and headed to the apartment building. He pretended to push a button on the door panel as the woman got to the steps.

"May I help you?"

"I'm here to see Leslie."

"She is not here now. She just left for a trip to New Haven for the day."

"Oh, so you know her then?"

"Oh yes, a very nice young lady. She lives across the hall from me. Would you like me to give her a message when she gets home?"

"You can tell her an old friend was in town and wanted to stop and surprise her. Let me hold the door for you."

"Can I get your name so I can tell her you were here."

"No, I want to surprise her. Just tell her a friend from school stopped by."

"I will give her the message when I see her" Mrs. Sester said as she put her key in the front door lock.

Tony held the door for her and watched her enter and go up the stairs. He put a piece of cardboard between the door and door-jam as it closed so it would not shut completely. He saw Mrs. Sester go into her apartment at the top of the stairs. He got into his car and drove around the block in case she was watching him leave. He parked a block away and walked back to the apartment building. He pushed the front door open, the cardboard dropped to the ground and he took the stairs two at a time to Leslie's apartment.

He put on a pair of rubber gloves he had in his back pocket especially for this occasion. It was an easy lock to pick and he was soon inside her apartment. Other than a box of papers and a book on the sofa, the apartment was as neat as a pin. He headed to the kitchen and opened the refrigerator. Not much in there. But he saw what he was looking for. There was a 2-liter bottle of soda sitting on the bottom shelf with about one glass of soda left in it. He took it out, put it on the counter and opened the top. He then removed a vial from his pocket and emptied the contents into the bottle. He then put the soda back into the refrigerator in the same place and facing the same way it was when he removed it moments ago.

The next person to have a taste of this soda will be the last taste they have of anything he thought to himself. He was hoping it would be Alex.

He left the apartment just as carefully as he entered it.

◆

Later that afternoon Leslie and Alex arrived back at her apartment.

"It is always good to get home, even after a day we had today."

"I know Leslie. It has been a very long day as well as a stressful one. How are you doing?"

"I'm fine Alex. Taking one step at a time as you said. At least we know that Sara is out there someplace and no one is playing a mean joke on you."

"Yes, we do."

Leslie grabbed Alex's hand and moved over to the sofa and sat down. He sat next to her.

"Alex, this has all been going too fast. All I have been thinking about is Sara and finding the truth. I haven't asked you how you feel?

You have been so helpful. I know you are doing this because of who you are. I don't know how you feel."

"Like you I am just a bundle of emotions right night. To tell the truth I don't know how I feel. As you said, things are happening so fast. All I know is that I want to make sure you are happy, and you are safe. Right now, that is all I can thank about. I know this is important to you and you need to find answers. The rest will have to wait until later. That is all I know."

"Thank you, Alex. I've put a lot pressure and stress on you. I didn't know what else to do."

"Don't worry. We are in this together. Now I need something to drink."

"I have some soda in the fridge. Let me get it for you" Leslie said as she headed to the kitchen.

She pulled a glass out of the cupboard and got the soda out of the refrigerator. She unscrewed the top and was just about to empty the contents into a glass when she heard a knock at the front door. Putting the soda down she headed to the door.

"Hello Mrs. Sester. Come on in. It is always good to see you."

"Thank you dear. I don't want to bother you."

"You are never a bother. We just got back from New Haven. It was a lovely day to take a ride in the country.

"Hi Alex."

"Hi Mrs. Sester. As Leslie said, it is always good to see you. You have always been so kind to us."

"I didn't want to bother you, but I promised to deliver you a message."

"What kind of message."

"A man stopped by this morning and said he was in town and wanted to surprise you. He said he went to school with you."

"Did he give you his name?"

"That was the strange thing. He didn't give me his name and I got the feeling he didn't want to give it to me. Just said he was a classmate and wanted to surprise you."

"Thank you so much, but I can't think of anyone from school that knows where I live that would want to surprise me."

"There was also something else strange about him."

"What is that?" Leslie asked

"He seemed so much older than you. Remember, look at the hands. His hands looked like he was 15-20 years older than you. But then again, I'm not good with guessing a person's age. At my age everyone looks young."

Suddenly Alex good really interested in the conversation. Up until then he was only half listening.

"Can you describe him to us, Mrs. Sester?"

'Well, he was a little shorter than you. His face was round, and he had dark brown hair."

"How was the hair cut?" Alex asked.

"It was very short…like they wear in the army?"

"Was he thin, average or fat."

"He wasn't thin or fat. But he did have a slight belly on him, like my husband. My husband, he liked his beer."

"Did you notice anything special about him. The way he walked or held his head, or anything that stood out in your mind. Anything special about the way he dressed?"

"Let's see. He was wearing brown pants and a blue shirt."

Alex heard a gasp come from Leslie.

"Did you notice anything unusual about his neck?" Alex continued.

"Why yes, he had a mole on the right side of his neck."

Alex looked at Leslie.

"Tony Neuman!" she said to no one in particular.

"Then you do remember him?" Mrs. Sester said. "Did you go to school with him?"

"No" Leslie said.

"I hope I didn't spoil the surprise. He insisted that he wanted to surprise you. Maybe you can pretend when you see him again."

"Yes. we will" Alex said as he led Mrs. Sester to the door. "thank you so much for delivering us the message.

Alex closed the door behind Mrs. Sester and turned to Leslie. "He is back in town and was here? I wonder if he was in the apartment?"

They both looked around to see if anything were out of place.

"What do we do now?" Leslie asked.

"I'm going to call the district attorney and let her know that we think Tony is back in town and see what she says."

"I thought this was all behind us."

"It will never be behind us until they catch him, and he is put away in prison. We just must continue on."

"You are right. What a bad hostess I am. I was about to get you something to drink" Leslie said and headed to the kitchen to get the soda. She needed to do something, anything or she would fall apart.

Alex took out his wallet to get the phone number of the District Attorney. She had written her private number on the back of her card.

Leslie picked up the bottle of soda she left on the counter to pour the contents into the glass sitting next to it. She turned to see Alex dialing his phone.

Turning back to the soda, she remarked to herself. "Damn, I left the top off when I went to answer the door. The fizz is all gone."

She walked to the sink, emptied the contents down the drain and threw the bottle into the trash and returned to the living room.

"I'm sorry Alex. That was the last of the soda that I have."

"Don't worry. I'll just have a glass of water."

Leslie returned to the kitchen, filled a glass with ice and returned to Alex.

"Hello, Ms. Fisher. This is Alex Gregory."

"Hello, Dr. Gregory. What can I do for you?"

"I think that Tony Neuman is back in New York and was as Leslie's apartment today."

"What makes you think that?"

Alex told her about the guy looking for Leslie and the description Mrs. Sester provided.

"Yes, it sounds like Tony Neuman. You stay there. I am calling the police to have someone come to watch your apartment again. Are you at home?"

"No, I'm at Leslie's place in Brooklyn Heights. I plan on spending the night here."

I will send a police car there immediately. Do not go leave the building."

"Please, no policemen. We will be careful. We don't want to feel trapped. We thank you for your offer."

"I don't feel comfortable with you two alone and Mr. Neuman back in the city."

"We will be careful and make sure we are never alone when we go out. We will stick to populated areas.

"Okay…but if you feel you are being watched or harassed please give me a call. We need you alive for the trial."

"We will be careful, and I promise to call if something feels out of place. We just don't want to feel like we are in a fish tank. I hope you understand."

"Okay, but if I get any information that might lead to your harm, I will have you watched by the police, fish tank or not."

"Fair enough."

The phone went dead. Alex turned to Leslie. She was standing there holding his glass of water, a look of fear on her face. Her hand was shaking, the ice hitting the sides of the glass. Alex took the glass and pulled Leslie over to the sofa. Putting the glass on the coffee table he sat down next to her. They both sat on the sofa. Before long Leslie was snuggling up against Alex.

"Will you spend the night Alex?"

"You don't have to ask twice" he said as he got up, took Leslie by the hand, and led her into the bedroom. "But first I want to take a shower...want to join me?" he said with a smirk on his face.

"You don't have to ask twice."

Chapter 22

*A*lex turned over in bed and quickly realized that he was alone. He lay back closing his eyes, taking in a few more minutes of sleep. Sunday is the day you should be able to sleep in. Then the aroma of coffee caused him to have second thoughts about sleeping in. It was drawing him to the kitchen. He swung his legs over the edge of the bed. Putting on his boxer shorts, he headed to the kitchen. He found Leslie putting a bagel in the toaster. He put his arms around her and kissed her on the neck.

"I heard you get up so put bagels in the toaster. It will be ready in a couple of minutes. But it will just have to be butter. I don't have any cream cheese" she said snuggling up against him. "And a hot cup of coffee to go with it."

"How did you sleep?" he asked.

"Kind of restless. But it would have been worse if you hadn't been here."

"Part of my charm" he responded, taking the cup of coffee Leslie was holding for him. He headed to the living room and sat down on the sofa, feet on the coffee table enjoying his coffee.

"You sure look comfortable."

"I could get used to this treatment."

"Don't get used to it. You need to pull your own weight in this relationship. I do like taking care of you. I also have to admit that you look good in just your boxers" she said with a wink.

"Whenever you want me like this, just say so."

"If I did that, we would surely get arrested…at least you would. And then there wouldn't be any surprise for me, when you take them off" she said winking at him.

"We had a great adventure yesterday. Let's relax today, unless you have something you want to do."

"I wouldn't call it an adventure. Yesterday was a long stressful day. I think we just need to stay in, watch some old movies and relax. Thank you again for staying by my side."

"No other place to go. I know what we can do today. Sit together and watch football."

"Let's stick to the old movies."

"I was planning on doing my laundry, but your idea is much better, even if it is watching old movies."

Leslie sat next to Alex on the sofa, her legs curled up under her, holding her coffee cup with both hands. "I just can't get over everything that happened and everything we found out yesterday."

"It was a lot…I'm almost on overload."

"My father must have been going through hell all these years. I'm sure it is a relief to him to get it out. But now he has to deal with mom."

"I'm sure they will work it out, but it might take a while. You just have to be patient."

"I wonder how much sleep they got last night?"

"Probably the same as you."

"Half the mystery is solved. We have to finish it" she said looking straight at Alex.

"Yes, we must, and we will. But remember, the police worked on it for years and couldn't find anything. So, we have to be realistic about our expectations and face the fact that we may never find anything more."

"I have faith in you Alex. Look what you found out about Sterling."

"I didn't do that alone. Most of the credit must be given to Cindy. She started the ball rolling and we had lots of supporting documents. Don't forget Brianna and what she did."

"Yes, Brianna. Without the documents she gave us and her warning, we might not be here. Even though I didn't know her well, I do think of her often. We might have become good friends."

"Yes, she was a wonderful woman. A shame that her life ended so early."

"You have the documents that my father gave you about the search for the kidnappers. Now you can do your stuff so we can find Sara."

"That is not the same Leslie. But I am curious as to what is in the folder your father gave me. Maybe that is how we spend today since we aren't going out."

"Like Sherlock Holmes."

"Let me go shower and put some clothes on first" Alex responded.

"I've already showered. You go shower but don't worry if you don't put on any clothes. I like you the way you are now. You look sexy in your boxers."

"This is how I am usually dressed when home alone on the weekend."

"Remind me to give you a surprise visit on the weekend."

"But if I don't get dressed now, we wouldn't get anything done" he said as he got up and headed to the bathroom.

"Leslie heard the shower and Alex humming as she stood at the kitchen sink washing the dishes. *Well, he sounded happy* she thought to herself. Then her thoughts went to the events of yesterday.

Leslie finished the dishes, went to the desk in the living room and pulled out the note that Mrs. Sester delivered to her. She sat back on the sofa and just looked at it. Alex returned from the bedroom with the folder that Leslie's dad gave him of the police investigation of the kidnapping.

"I can't believe that is all she wrote. 'YOUR DAUGHTER SARA NEEDS YOU!' What did she expect to happen?"

"She may not have thought it through or was in a hurry. We can only guess."

"Another strange thing. If you were going to kidnap a baby, wouldn't you at least change the name so it couldn't be traced?

"I would think so, but we won't know the answer to that and the hundred other questions we have until we find her."

"Then you want to find her too?" Leslie asked.

"Of course, I do. I am in this as much as you are. You know how much I like a good mystery. But more importantly, I know how much this means to you."

"Thank you" Leslie responded, stroking his arm.

"Okay, let's see what's in all these files your father gave me" Alex said as he started to lay out the papers on the table. "Let's sort them by date so we can follow the sequence of events."

They spent the next half hour organizing the documents.

"Here is the first report by the police. They interviewed everyone at the hospital and concluded that no one in the hospital was involved. They surmised that the person came from the outside and waited for the right opportunity. Also, since they didn't find any fingerprints, they concluded that it was a professional job by someone who know what he or she was doing. Also, all the cameras had been sprayed with black paint. This means that this was a well-planned operation."

"I never thought it could have been a woman. I just assumed it was a man who did the kidnapping" Leslie said looking at Alex.

"The police first thought it might have been a woman, since women are the ones that usually steal babies from hospitals. Because of the professional job, they thought it was probably a man, but never ruled out the possibility of a woman."

They spent the next two hours going through all the documents.

"Nothing stands out to me. The police spent a lot of time and manhours trying to solve this" Alex said turning to Leslie. He saw disappointment on her face.

"I'm was sure we would find something."

"The police are professionals, Leslie."

Leslie picked up the note again and read it. "Why didn't she say more" she said under her breath.

"I'm sorry Leslie."

Alex reached over and took the note from Leslie's hand. Like her he read it again and again, looking for some type of clue. Nothing...

Suddenly, Alex stopped and held the note up in the air, the light from the window shining through the paper.

"Did you find something?" Leslie asked.

Silence...

Leslie asked again, "Do you see something?"

"There are some water marks on the paper. I'm trying to figure out what they say. Do you have a magnifying glass?"

Leslie went to the desk and brought back a magnifying glass. Alex held the paper up to the light and read the water marks.

"It is the name of the store who made this paper. The name of the shop is Dempts and Marlow. There are some numbers on the stationery. It could be a stock number or if the stationary is custom made, the numbers could lead us to the person who ordered the stationery."

Alex got his phone and did a search for the stationery shop.

"It is on 58th and Second Avenue."

He dialed the number from the website".

Leslie sat there tensely watching Alex.

He turned off his phone and looked at Leslie. "I got a voice recording that they are closed on Sunday. The message also said that they produced customized stationery."

"Then they are still in business" Leslie said.

"This is a start Leslie. We can go there after work tomorrow and see if they can give us the name of the person who ordered this stationery."

"The hunt continues" Leslie responded throwing her arms around Alex. "I knew you would solve this for me."

"Don't thank me yet. This could just as easy be a dead end. But I like the hug. She gave him another hug, longer and harder.

"Now what do we do for the rest of the day?" he said with a wink.

"An old movie and an early dinner. We will then see what comes up" she said looking at Alex' boxers.

Chapter 23

*L*eslie was already waiting in the lobby when Alex arrived after work the next day.

"Have you been waiting long?"

"About three minutes. We probably left at the same time. But I have an express elevator" Leslie responded, referring to the executive private elevator she has access to.

"It is so nice out and the printer's shop is only 14 blocks away. Let's walk rather than take the subway. We will probably get there faster" Alex stated.

"Let's go" Leslie said, putting her hand on Alex's arm."

They walked uptown to 58th street and crossed Park Avenue heading east toward Second Avenue. Dempts and Marlow was on the corner. The store had a painted gray brick front with a lavender awning bearing their name. A large window displayed all types of paper products alone with a large display of writing pens, including several with feathers. On the side of front door was a plaque imprinted with 'Family Business Since 1960.'

Alex and Leslie entered the store. A bell rang as they opened the door announcing a customer. A young girl was behind a counter wrapping a gift for a waiting customer. She looked up as the bell rang. She was in her 20s with large wire framed glasses on her round face.

"I'll be with you in a minute" and then returned to wrapping the package.

There was a display of customer stationery on one wall. Alex moved closer to the display pointing out the water mark on each of the sheets of paper. They all had the same mark as the one on Leslie's paper, except the number was different. Just then, Alex heard the bell ring and looked toward to the door and saw the customer leaving with the wrapped package in her hand. The salesperson moved up behind Alex.

"May I help you?"

"I saw the plaque that this store has been in the family since 1960. Are you a member of the family? Alex asked setting up a friendly rapport with the clerk.

"Yes, the store is run by my grandfather. I work here on days when I'm not in class."

"Where do you take classes?"

"I'm a student at Columbia University."

"That is in my neighborhood. I live on the Upper West Side, just 15 blocks from Columbia. It has a beautiful campus. What are you studying?"

"This is my third year. I'm majoring in economics."

"Well, good luck to you.

"Thank you very much. Is there something that I can help you with?"

"Are all these stationery samples made by this store?" Alex asked pointing to the sample stationary displayed.

"Yes, we are very proud of our custom stationery business. Are you interested in a customized stationery?"

"We received a note on stationery with a water mark like those on these samples. We just want to verify that this paper was produced by you. We liked the quality of the paper."

"May I see the paper?"

Alex folded the paper so the water mark showed but the message was covered and handed it to the clerk."

She took the paper and held it up to the light.

"Yes, we made this stationery. It has our logo and item number embedded in the paper. Do you wish to reorder?"

"No. We just would like to know who ordered this paper. Are you able to tell from the water mark?"

"The number under the water mark identifies the person who ordered the paper. Let me check our records."

Leslie grabbed Alex's arm with excitement.

The clerk went behind the desk and pulled out a large book from a shelf under the counter. She opened the book and turned to the page that had the specific item number.

"I'm sorry, I am not able to give you the name of the person. Some of our customers have asked not to have their identity revealed. The customer has requested that. Can I ask why you need to know the person's identity?"

"I really like the quality of this paper. It has the right combination of paper fiber and linen. I want to get a larger order of this quality for my company."

"I could have some made for you, since we have formula here."

"Thank you, but I wouldn't feel right using someone else's formula without their permission. It goes against my business principles." Alex was making this up as he went along hoping it would convince the clerk to provide the name or address of the customers. At the time he was trying to read the address of the customer from the book in front of the clerk. The writing was too small to read upside down. But he did notice that she had her finger on the 6th entry from the top of the page. And the page number was in very large print and it was page 57. He turned his eyes away from the book.

"I'm sorry sir, I can't go against company policy."

"I understand."

Alex turned to Leslie who was standing behind him. "I want to show you something." He turned and walked to a display on another wall, out of the earshot of the clerk.

"Call the clerk over to ask a question. Make sure her back is to the front desk."

"Excuse me. Can you help me with some questions I have about this item?" Leslie said pointing to the display near the front window.

The clerk left the front counter and moved to Leslie. Leslie started asking her questions about the make of the paper and anything else she could think of, making sure the clerk's back was to the front desk.

Alex quietly moved to the front desk. The client book was still out, opened to the page. He leaned over the desk and took several pictures of the page in the book with his cell phone. Then he quietly moved back to stand behind the clerk, as if he had been there all the time.

"You have been very helpful in explaining the difference types of paper that you offer. We will have to think about it and come back once we have made a decision."

"Yes, thank you very much" Alex added standing close to the clerk to give the impression that he had been there all time. "We really appreciate your time. You have very high-quality paper and high integrity when it comes to the request of your customers. That is very important to us."

"Alex let's go get dinner and talk about our visit here. I see a Mexican restaurant across the street. I'm in the mood for a taco salad" Leslie said pointing to the restaurant across the street, a restaurant she had notice as she was looking out the window. Dinner was a good excuse to leave the paper store.

With that the two of them left the store and headed to the restaurant.

"A burrito sounds good" Alex said as he opened the door to the Mexican restaurant.

Leslie turned as she entered the building and saw the clerk standing in the window watching them. Alex and Leslie were fortunate to get a table by a window inside the restaurant. The clerk was no longer watching them and had moved back to her counter, probably to put the book away. Alex looked up from his menu.

"I think I will have a burrito and beer. What looks good to you?

"I think I talked myself into the taco salad. It was the first thing that came to my mind while I was talking to the clerk."

The waiter came over and Alex gave him their order.

"So, did you get the information from the Customer Book?"

"I've been waiting until we were not being interrupted to see what I got." Alex took out his phone and opened the photos. Scrolling through he found the pictures he took of the page in the book. Enlarging the picture, he saw the record that corresponded to number on the piece of paper. "I got the address…18 Widow Coopers, Sag Harbor, Long Island. There is no name associated with that address. Let me check the internet and see if I can find a name associated with that address."

Leslie watched intently as Alex went through several sites looking for the owner of the home. Their food came and was placed on the table. Neither of them started eating. Leslie watched as Alex continued checking various sites.

"I couldn't find a name anyplace. The home is registered to a corporation and I can't find anything more than the name of the corporation. It must be a shell company to cover up the name of the owner."

"Maybe the mob" Leslie said.

"You've been watching too many gangster movies."

"Let me go into Google Map and see if we can get a picture of the house."

Alex punched a few more keys.

"Wow, this is a huge house. Here is a picture of it. Maybe you are right, and it is a mob house. Look at the high wall around the house and the iron gate across the driveway" Alex said showing the picture to Leslie.

"It is large. I can't believe Sara would need me, living in a house like that. What does it say about the house? Any history?"

"You never know what goes on behind the walls in a large house or a small house. All it says is that the house is owned by a corporation, it is over 9,000 square feet with 6 bedrooms and 6 bathrooms. It was built in 1982 and has an estimate value of six million dollars."

"Since we don't know the owner and can't call, I guess we will just need to take a trip to Long Island."

"You always seem to surprise me Leslie, with your wild ideas. Now, let's eat."

Chapter 24

*T*he salesgirl was not the only one watching Alex and Leslie enter the Mexican restaurant. Tucked back in the shadows of a doorway a few stores down from the paper store, stood Tony Neuman, watching every move the two made after they left the stationery shop.

Enjoy your meal, Alex…it could be your last he thought to himself.

Tony has been watching Alex for many days, trying to understand his routine. He needed to find a time and place to eliminate Alex quickly and quietly. This thought was constantly on his mind…*How can I get rid of Alex Gregory, the guy who put me in prison? The person responsible for my situation. May he rot in hell.*

After he had doctored the soda at Leslie's apartment, he waited outside her apartment expecting an ambulance or police car to arrive with sirens blaring. He waited until past midnight and nothing. That was his first try to get Alex, but not his last. Now to come up with another plan.

He had not been sleeping well and knew that he would not until this was behind him. With Alex gone he could head south and finally get a good night's sleep, away from New York and from the police. He had his bags all packed, ready to head to the airport on a moment's notice. He would have to get out of the area quickly. He had moved out of the uptown apartment to a place closer to the airport for a quick escape when the time came to leave. He had decided not to fly out of a major airport. He didn't want to take the chance that they were being watched, although he saw no signs of it. Even with his fake ID's he didn't want to take a chance. He would leave from MacArthur Airport on Long Island. He would fly from there to Philadelphia and then on to South America. He was already imaging siting on a beach living on all the money had he stored away in an offshore account. He would be there now if it hadn't been for Alex Gregory.

He was glad that the police were no longer escorting Alex around. They must think that he is still in Canada. His plan worked. One less obstacle in his way. Since following Alex, he had not been able to establish a routine for him. Maybe he doesn't have a routine, or he needs more time to find Alex's routine. But time is something he did not have. All he knew is that he wanted it over so he could get on with his life.

Damn, why didn't the poison in the soda work. It would have been so cool to watch from a distance. Watching the police and fire trucks arrive at the house. Men running around. Sitting in his car waiting for a body to be brought down the stairs. But nothing happened? Damn Alex…why didn't you drink the soda.

Tony continued to stand in the doorway, pushed back into the corner so not to be seen, down the street from the Mexican restaurant. He could see the two of them sitting in the window. He watched them order and then saw Alex take out his cell phone and start pushing keys.

What a dope he thought. *Sitting there with a beautiful woman and he is on his phone.* He continued to watch as their food arrived, and they ate. Alex still on his phone.

He started to feel hunger pains but didn't want to leave. A plan was forming in his mind as he continued to watch. He hoped that no one would wonder why he was standing there all alone for so long. Then again, this is New York City and people avoid making eye contact or acknowledge people on the street. They are also so used to seeing strange happenings that nothing seems unusual. He once remembered walking down the Lexington Avenue and saw a man standing looking in the window of Bloomingdales talking to the person in the window. The only person in the window was his own reflection. He was cursing the guy in the window for not answering his questions. People walked by, took a glance at the guy, then continued walking, but at a faster pace. People then looked back to see if they were being followed. Tony did the same.

He again looked at the restaurant. Alex was no longer at the table in the window. Was so wrapped up in his own thoughts that he didn't see them leave their table? Tony looked up and down the street to make sure he hadn't missed him as he was daydreaming. Just then the door to the restaurant opened and Alex and Leslie stepped out. A few steps away from the restaurant, Alex took Leslies hand. She didn't resist.

How sweet he thought. *Enjoy it while you can. You won't have his hand to hold much longer. Except holding it when he dies in front of you.*

He watched then head back the same way they came, still hand in hand. He was behind them across the street. It is easier to blend in and not be noticed when on the opposite street. How happy they seemed, just talking, and not noticing him. Well, that won't last long.

They arrived at the entrance of the subway shuttle in Grand Central Station, Alex stepping aside to let Leslie go first. He followed behind her and then through the turn style down another set of stairs to wait for the train. Since this was the dinner hour the platform was full of people; those catching the train on the way home after work, and those heading to happy hour before dinner.

Tony raced down the stairs keeping his distance but didn't want to lose Alex in the crowd. He could see him up ahead, moving toward the middle of the platform. This was going to be easy. With all the people around, he could walk up to Alex, pull out his gun, put a bullet in him and then blend in with the crowd. In the commotion he would quietly go up the stairs and leave the subway. Then home, grab his bag and passport and off to the airport.

A train was approaching. That is even better. Everyone was looking away from him, watching the train slowly pull into the station. That way he could move up to Alex without being observed. Move up behind Alex with people getting on and getting off the subway. More people, more commotion, easier escape. He pushed his way through the crowd closer to Alex.

Tony slowly reached into his pocket, putting his hand around his gun as he got closer. This was going to be easy. He felt a person brush against him. He automatically turned to see who it was. Then he saw two policemen about twenty feet away moving in his direction, patrolling the platform, watching the people get off the train. He released his hand from the gun and slowly pulled his hand out of his pocket. He remembered a news report that crime on the subway was on the rise. As a result, the mayor had requested that more uniform policemen patrol the subways. The doors of the subway opened, and people pushed their way out. With all the people entering and leaving the subway, the two policemen turned to watch the people leaving and entering the subway car. They were only about five feet away from Tony. He watched Alex and Leslie push their way into the subway. He didn't want to get on the subway. A subway car was no place to shoot someone…no escape route. Also, the train was so packed with people that he would not have been able to get close to Alex. So, he stood back as if waiting for the next train to arrive.

The subway doors closed, and the train started down the track to the next station. Out of the corner of his eye he saw the two policemen continue down the platform. There were few people standing on the platform now. As the subway car passed him, he saw Alex and Leslie standing in the aisle. Alex's back was to him. Leslie seemed to be looking right at him through the windows After the train left Tony turned and left the subway, exiting the opposite direction of the policemen.

Did Leslie recognize him? If she did, they would be on their guard and the police protection would be back in place. Damn, now what does he do. He would have to come up with another plan.

Chapter 25

"*A*lex, I think I just saw Tony Neuman" Leslie said, a look of fear on her face.

Alex turned toward the window, but the subway had just left the station.

"Are you sure?"

"Not one hundred percent sure but it surely looked like him."

"If it is him, then he has been following us."

"I'm worried Alex. That is twice he has found us."

"We have to call the District Attorney. We can't take a chance anymore and try to protect ourselves."

The train pulled into the station at Time Square. Alex pulled out his cell phone and called the District Attorney's private number.

"Hello Ms. Fisher. This is Alex Gregory. I'm sorry to bother you, but there is a possibility that Tony Neuman is not in Canada, but in New York and is following us. Leslie thinks she saw him standing on the subway platform in Grand Central as the train we were on left the station."

"Where are you?"

"We are on the subway platform in Time Square. We were heading home, Leslie to Brooklyn and me to the Upper West Side."

"There is a police station in Time Square at 43rd Street and 7th avenue, just a block from where you are. Go there now. A policeman will meet you there. I'm calling them now." The phone went dead.

Alex and Leslie entered the station and walked up to the counter.

"May I help you?" the office behind the desk asked.

"We were told to come here by the District Attorney's office. A police officer is supposed to meet us here. My name is Alex Gregory."

"Yes, we did receive a call from the DA's office. Please take a seat. The officer will be here shortly."

Fifteen minutes later a man approached them. Alex recognize him. It was the same policeman that had been assigned to him before.

"Good evening officer. It is good to see you again."

"Good to see you too. Time to get you home and safe."

"We need to make a stop on the way."

Alex turned to Leslie.

"You are moving in with me. I don't want you alone. I want to make sure you are safe. We will go by your place, pack your things and then back to my apartment. My place has a doorman. No one can get in without being announced. I won't take no for an answer. I'm concerned about you."

With that, the three of them left the train station and headed to Leslie's place in Brooklyn. Not much was said during the trip, but Leslie held Alex's hand very tightly.

"It will be about 30 minutes" Alex said as he got out of the car, holding the door for Leslie.

"I'll be right here. Do you still have my phone number?" "Yes, right here in my head" Alex said as he recited the number.

"We'll call when we are ready to leave Thank you officer." With that Alex shut the car door and joined Leslie at the front door of her building.

"Are you sure this is necessary, Alex?" Leslie asked as she unlocked the door to her apartment.

"You know that if you were here alone, I would worry about you all the time. This way I know you are safe. I also don't want you to be worrying about me…I assume you would" he said with a wink.

With that Leslie went into the bedroom, pulled out a suitcase and started to fill it. Alex just stood in the doorway and watched.

"How much should I pack. I will need work clothes, casual, make-up. You know it is more difficult for a woman than a man."

"Pack for three to four days. If we need anything else, we can always come by and get them. Afterall, we have a chauffeur at our disposal. And think how much fun it will be living together."

"Haven't we been doing that already? I think I've lived more with you the past two months than I've lived alone,"

"You don't hear me complaining. Nice to have my coffee all made for me in the morning when I wake up."

"Don't let that become a habit. New rule…first person up makes the coffee for the one still in bed" she responded.

"Good reason for me to stay in bed in the morning."

"Is that the only reason?"

"I could think of a few others."

"Well, I think I have everything" Leslie said closing her suitcase. "Let me go across the hall and have Mrs. Sester pick up my mail. I don't want my mailbox downstairs to overflow. And she doesn't mind doing that for me."

Alex called the policeman and told him they were leaving now. He picked up the suitcases and met Leslie at her door. She was just saying thank you to Mrs. Sester.

Back in the police car they headed back to Manhattan. Forty minutes later they were walking into his apartment. It was after eleven and time to go to bed.

"This has been a long day Alex. I'm so tired. I just want to shower and go to bed."

"I'll shower when you are finished."

As Leslie showered, Alex checked his messages and answered a few texts. He stood in the window looking out at the lights of New Jersey across the Hudson River. So much has happened today. Besides a full day of work, they found out the address of the person who had purchased the paper that the note was written on. Then after a nice dinner they realized that Tony Neuman might be back in New York City and following them again. Or it could have been a mistake, someone who looked like Tony. Hard to be absolutely sure when you only see as figure through a moving subway window.

If he had been following them, how long has this been going on. He was at Leslie apartment building recently based on the description from Mrs Sester. So much has happened the past two days.

"I'm finished" Leslie said a she entered the room wearing his bathrobe. "I hope you don't mind if I put this on. I found it on the back of the door, and I didn't bring anything with me."

"You can wear it as often as you want. In fact, you look better in it than I do" he said, giving her a kiss on the check as he headed to take a shower.

Like Alex, Leslie moved to the window looking at the view as she remembered the events of the past couple of days. Sara had been kidnaped and they found the address of the person who sent the messages. *Where is she? Is she okay? What has she been told?* So many questions went through her head.

"Nice view isn't it?"

Leslie turned to see Alex standing there with only a towel around his waist and drying his hair with another. He placed the towel around his neck and moved behind Leslie, putting his arms around her waist. They both just stood there looking at the nights light and the lights of a barge moving up the Hudson River.

"What do we do now, Alex?"

"I've been thinking about that. Let's go sit." They moved to the sofa.

"I don't think either of us will rest until we find out where this note leads. I hate to take a day off work, but I think we need to do that tomorrow, rent a car and check out that address."

"Okay" Leslie responded with excitement in her voice.

"I see three possibilities when we get there. One…It could be the address of a home where the red hair woman lives or works, and the paper is the stationery of the family who lives there. Second…it could be a business and the red hair woman works there and somehow knows about Sara. Third…It could be a place that was once a business that used that stationery and has since moved to a new location and a house built on the property. The red hair lady may work at the new location or if the business is defunct, she may somehow have gotten some of the old stationery.

"If that is the case the people who now live in the house may know about the company and how to find the red headed woman" Leslie responded.

"And they may not know."

"We could also check with a realtor. They would have sales history."

"Remember there was no name associated with the address at the stationery shop, just a company's name and they didn't want their information shared. Sounds like they might have something to hide. I assumed it was a shell company for the owner of the house. The owner just may not want to be found. Also, we don't know how old that paper is. There was no date in the customer book as to when the paper was ordered."

"When we looked at Google Map, there was a house there, not a business. So, I would think that is what is there."

"Yes, it shows a house. But, the picture was taken in 2013 according to the data on the picture. Who knows that has happened since then?"

"So, I guess we have to go find out. You know Alex, this will bother both of us until we find the answer."

"You're right. Let's find out. One more piece of the puzzle."

"But how do we get there. Remember, we are not supposed to leave the building without a policeman. I'm sure they are outside the building right now."

Alex thought for a moment.

"How about this. We call the police in the morning and have them take us to work. Once we are there they will probably leave until we call them in the afternoon to take us home. We can stop in at Human Resources and tell them we will be taking the day off. They will not have any problem with that. We won't have to explain why we want to leave. They will assume it has something to do with the trial. We will then rent a car and drive out to Long Island and be back before work is over so the police will pick us up and take us home. It will appear that we have been at the office all day."

"As usually you have everything worked out."

"So, let's go to bed and get some sleep. But before that, I have some other activity to 'discuss'."

"I'll race you to be the bedroom."

Chapter 26

*T*he smell of coffee drew Leslie from the bedroom to the living room.

"See, I can make coffee, too. How did you sleep?"

"You can probably answer that question. Restless, but not as bad as the other time."

"Finish your coffee and let's get ready for work."

"It takes me longer than you, so let me shower first."

Leslie headed to the shower and Alex went to his computer to print out the directions to the address on Long Island. Google reported that it will take about 2 hours and 45 minutes. He studied the map.

If we leave work soon after we arrive, we should be there by noon. Check out the area for a couple of hours and then return back at the office in time to be escorted home and no one to the wiser.

Leslie came out of the bathroom and Alex went in. Twenty minutes later he was ready for work in his business casual. Alex called the number for the police car and fifteen minutes later they were on their way to office in the backseat of the police car.

They went to Human Resources and told them that they would be taking the day off for personal use. No one asked the purpose. They just said have a good day.

Twenty minutes later they were getting into the rental car on their way to Long Island. There was little talk on the way there. Leslie was deep in her thoughts and Alex was concentrating on driving. The Southern State Parkway wasn't crowded at this time of day, so he made good time. He exited onto Highway 27 heading to Sag Harbor.

"We need to talk about how we are going to approach this before we just show up. Like we did in New Haven. We have no idea what we are getting ourselves into" Alex said.

"As usual, you are right."

"Let's get off at the next exit and look for a place to eat. It is time for lunch and I'm hungry. I don't want to play Sherlock Holmes on an empty stomach. We don't want my growling stomach to give our position away."

"You come up with the strangest comments to lighten the moment. I will admit however, that they do work. I've been going over and over in my mind what might happen and how I might respond versus how I should respond to what we find today."

Alex turned off the expressway at the next exit and traveled a frontal road. About a half mile down the road, they saw **Itsi's Diner**.

"Must be a family name" Leslie remarked.

Alex pulled into the parking lot. It was about three quarters full.

"Must be a popular place" Alex remarked. "But then again it is lunch time."

When they entered, they felt that had stepped back tin the fifties. A customer counter ran along one wall with the typical round counter stools with no back of that period. Half of them were occupied with people eating. A waiter was behind the counter taking orders and picking up orders from the kitchen and placing them in front of the customer. There were booths along the wall and tables in the center. All the booths were occupied. Alex saw a table in the back and headed toward it as he heard someone come in behind him. Leslie followed.

The table was old with chips of the plywood missing on the side. There was a napkin holder in the center of the table with salt and pepper shakers next to it, a menu placed between them. Alex took a menu and handed it to Leslie. Just as she opened it a waitress placed a second menu on the table with two glasses of water.

"I'll be back in a minute to take your order."

"Now that is efficient. In New York you usually flag down someone to get water and usually wait for a table. I think I am in the mood for a Rueben with pastrami and iced tea. What looks good to you?"

"I'm just going to have a Caesar salad and tea."

The waitress returned, took their orders and left without a word or even a smile.

"So, what are your concerns Leslie? You said you didn't know how you would react."

"Up until now, this didn't seem entirely real. It seemed as if I were just walking through a dream. This is the first time that we might be close to an actual person. We might even meet the red hair woman."

"It will be nice to put a name to that person."

"If I meet Sara, I don't know what I will or should do. Do I tell her who I am? Or do I just say I'm a friend of the family just stopping by? What does she know and how do we find out what she knows? The red hair lady apparently believes she doesn't belong there."

"That is a lot for you to wrap your arms around in a short period of time. We have been on the go since you got that note. You haven't had time to sit back and digest all of this. Do you want to take some time and go back home and come back here another day?"

"One side of me says let's find out and get this over with...but another side is scared as to what will happen and says let's go home and put it off for another day."

"I will do whatever you want."

"Putting it off won't make it go away but will give me time to adjust to what is going on. But then again, if Sara needs my help, I need to be there for her and must go on no matter how I feel."

"That is your motherly instincts coming out...children always come first. I think we need to take this to the end, no matter where it takes us."

Silence

"I agree... let's go for it."

"As we said earlier there are three scenarios...first, we will find a residence at that location; second, there is a business there; third was a business that moved, and a house was built."

"So, what's the plan?"

"Let's assume the address is a home. Let's use the same plan we did in New Haven. You stay in the car and let me go up to the house and see if I can find out if there is a child there that is ten years. I'll use the same excuse. I'm collecting data on families with children for a research project conducted by a university. The project involves data on how families feel about getting their children vaccinated with the various children vaccines."

"You sound very professional."

"I'm making this up as I go along."

"Well, it sounds very professional to me."

"Are you ready? I'm finished but looks like you are still working on your salad."

"I'm not hungry. Let's go."

"Okay, let's pay the bill and get on our way. We are ten to fifteen minutes away."

They got back into the car and headed down the highway listening to the GPS for directions. As they approached the second offramp they were instructed to get off. Five minutes later they saw a street sign for Widow Coopers. Alex turned into the street.

"Now we need to find No. 18.

"Leslie had her face glued to the window. "It has to be on this side. These are even numbers."

Then they saw it. A large white mansion of light-yellow colored stone, a ten-foot hedge around the property with a driveway leading to a gate at the road. Alex drove past the property to three properties away and turn around so he could park across the street from the house. He purposely parked the car in such a way that they could see the front door.

"Now what do we do. Can't just walk up to the front door with the gate there."

"Maybe there is buzzer on the gate that we can ring and have someone come let us in" Leslie said.

"I don't think that will work" Alex replied pointing to the front gate. "There is a speaker box on the left side of the gate that you will need to talk into. I'm sure they are not going to let someone in who is there for a survey. If you look up, you will see that there are cameras pointing at the gate. I wouldn't be surprised that they can also see us sitting here now."

"Well, we at least know that it is a house rather than a business. Or it could have been a business at one time that was torn down and a house build on the property."

"I don't think that is the case. Look at the hedges and trees. This house has been here a long time. This is probably where your note came from. Now we just need to get in and see who lives there."

"Maybe we can wait down the street and watch the front gate out of the sight of the cameras?"

"That might work" Alex responded. "Except we may be here a long time and looking at the houses on this street, I'm sure they are patrolled."

"Then what is your suggestion, Mr. Holmes?"

Alex turned forward looking up the street trying to think of some scenarios. Leslie continued to look at the house

Sudden Alex heard "Oh My God" and turned toward Leslie. Her stare was frozen, and she looked very pale.

Alex looked at the house and responded softly "Oh My God."

Chapter 27

*T*hey both stared at the front door. While they were discussing their next plan, Leslie noticed the front door open and out stepped a woman wearing a white blouse and a pair of dark green slacks. As she turned back to the front door her flaming red hair wrapped around her head. She held the door open and out stepped a young girl about ten years of age.

"That has to be Sara" Leslie said under her breath.

Alex grabbed her hand as he continued to stare at the pair standing on the front steps of the house.

Sara jumped off the steps and started running around in the grassy area in the front of the house. The red hair woman stood on the steps watching her play, a smile on her face. Leslie watched every move that Sara made. The woman turned her head toward their car and just stared at it. She could not have seen them. They were too far away. Then she did something strange. She started walking toward the gate, leaving Sara to play in the yard.

"Stay in the car. I am going to go talk to her. Give me the note."

Leslie reached into her purse and handed the note to Alex. He left the car and headed to the gate. By this time, the red hair woman was at the gate looking through the iron grid.

"Are you looking for someone? she asked as Alex reached the gate. "No one ever parks across the street, so I assume you are looking for someone or for some place. Maybe I can help."

Alex open the note that he had in his hand and handed it to the woman. "Did you write this?"

The woman took the note, looked at it and then gave it back to Alex. Then she looked toward the car and saw Leslie sitting there.

"Who are you? she asked.

My name is Alex Gregory and the woman in the car behind me is a friend. This note was delivered to her place in Brooklyn. Did you deliver it there?"

With the mention of his name there was an expression of fear on her face.

"There are camera's watching us. No one is home right now, but they will be returning soon. I am the nanny here, hired to take care of the child."

Alex thought, *why did she say **the** child rather than **their** child?*

"Very beautiful child" Alex said. "What is her name?"

"Sara."

With that statement, Alex was sure that the child was the missing Sara, Leslie's daughter.

"Can we meet later. I can meet you at three someplace else so we can talk."

"Do you know **Itsie's Diner** along the expressway two exits back? We will be there at three."

"Yes, I know it. I'll see you there" she said handing the note back to Alex and starting back toward the house. She looked over her shoulder and said, "I'm glad you came."

Alex stood and watched as the woman call Sara and they both disappeared into the house. Alex returned to the car. Leslie was sitting there, her stare frozen on his face.

"What happened?"

"The girl's name is Sara." He watched for her reaction. It was not what he expected. All she did was smile and tears formed in her eyes.

"There is more, Leslie. I showed the woman the note and the reaction I got from her confirmed that she did deliver the note to you. But she was anxious and did not want to talk anymore or hang around. We arranged a meeting at Itsie's at three o'clock. There was a look of concern on her face."

"Then something is wrong?"

The happy face turned to one of concern.

"As she left, she turned and thanked us for coming."

Leslie looked at her watch. "That is a little more than an hour from now. What do we do until then?

"First of all, let us get out of this neighborhood. I don't want to be stopped by a patrol car asking what we are doing here."

Alex started the car and headed back toward the highway.

"This is such a beautiful area. Let's just drive around and take in the big mansions and treelined streets.

For the next hour they drove up and down the streets taking in the picturesque streets of Long Island, lined with one mansion after the other, each trying to impress their neighbors and display their wealth. At 2:45 they were pulling into the parking lot of the diner. There were only three other cars there, so the diner was empty this time of day. They took a booth toward the back so they would be out of earshot of people around. Alex ordered a coffee and piece of chocolate cake and Leslie got a pot of tea.

"You can't resist your sweets can you."

"When it comes to chocolate, especially chocolate cake with chocolate frosting, I can't say no."

Alex was finishing up his cake when Leslie nodded toward the front door and said, "She's here."

Alex turned to the door and motioned the red hair woman to the booth. She slid in next to Leslie.

"Thank you for meeting with us" Alex said. "You must have been surprised at our arrival. First, can I ask you name."

"I'm sorry. I'm Rebecca."

"I'm Alex and this is Leslie. Nice to finally meet you."

"To answer your next question, I've been expecting you to arrive ever since I delivered that note to you. I have been watching for someone to show up at the estate. When I saw you parked across the street I was thinking, you might be who I was looking for."

"Thank you for reaching out to us. All these years I thought that Sara died in the hospital. That is what everyone told me and what I have been living with. Now I know my daughter is alive."

Leslie leaned over and gave Rebecca a hug.

"I had to, for Sara's sake."

"Is something wrong" Leslie asked staring wide-eyed at Rebecca.

"No, I didn't mean to frighten you. Sara is fine."

"I'm so glad."

"Why didn't you leave an address on the note" Alex asked.

"I had to make sure you were interested in finding her. If you showed up, then I knew you were concerned an serious and would do everything you could to find her."

"You said she is happy. Why would you risk that by contacting me?"

"I said she was fine...I didn't say she was happy. She is a very lovely child, but not a happy child. She is not allowed to be a child or have friends. They take care of her but I'm not sure if they love her. But her grandfather adores her. He is a very powerful man. I think they had the child for his sake."

"How did you find me and why now?" Leslie asked.

Alex noticed her hands and based on Mrs. Sester's theory he surmised that Rebecca was in her mid fifties.

"Let me go back a little and bring you up to date. Then everything will fit together. "It is not a happy story, nor is it sad, but it is a story that you need to hear."

"Please" Leslie said, continuing to stare at Rebecca to make sure she didn't miss anything.

Chapter 28

"*I* have been working for the family for eighteen years. I was hired as a housekeeper, but later became the full-time nanny for Sara. Sara's grandfather owns the house. It is his daughter who is the mother…. I'm sorry, I mean the adopted mother" she said as she looked at Leslie. "Her name is Maria."

Alex and Leslie looked intently at Rebecca, taking in every word.

"Maria and her husband, Nick had tried for years to get pregnant, but it was not in the cards. Maria's grandfather suggested and convinced them to try a surrogate. The grandfather is a very persuasive man. Essentially, he gets what he wants. No one says no to him. His wife died 6 years ago. She was the only person I ever saw stand up to him."

"That has to be a difficult place to live" Alex added.

"It is. Everyone walks as if on eggshells whenever he was in the house. I think that Nick was afraid of the grandfather and did everything he asked without question. He and Maria moved into the house after they were married and live in a separate wing. You saw how big the house is. It has everything that you expect of a house this size…large lawn, swimming pool in the back and a tennis court. There is a separate guest house for visitors at the end of the property way in the back. Anyone there will feel like that are not part of the estate it is so far away. Over the years people have come and gone from that guest house. I never know when someone is there. The lights are on all the time, even when no one is there. They are all on timers and go on and off all day and night as if someone is there, even when it is empty."

"So, about ten years ago, they found a surrogate to carry their baby?" Alex asked.

"Well, yes and no" Rebecca answered.

Alex and Leslie looked puzzled.

"We were all told that Nick and Maria had found a surrogate. The grandfather was very happy. They went about getting the baby's room ready. There was a lot of joy in the house. About a month before the birth of the child there was change in Maria and Nick. The happiness stopped. No one knew why. Then about a month later Nick and Maria went to the hospital and came home with a baby girl. They named the baby Sara. Everyone thought that the surrogate delivered on her promise. It was now a happy home again."

"My baby? Leslie asked, tears forming in her eyes.

"Yes, but we didn't know it at the time."

"How did you find out?" Alex asked.

"The years passed by and the family went about their normal lives. The grandfather was extremely happy to have his grandchild. It was as if the child was his. He worshipped her and took over all the decision about her. Her care was turned over to me. It was as if Nick and Maria had no say in Sara's life."

"So, Sara was safe and happy?" Leslie asked.

"Yes, she was safe, but I don't think happy. It was not a happy environment. Yes, she was spoiled and had everything she wanted. But she was not allowed to go out, have close friends or even go to school. She was home schooled. Not by a family member, but by a teacher hired for that purpose."

Rebecca looked at Leslie. "Here comes the hard part."

"The week before her 10th birthday the family went to New York City for the weekend to celebrate the holidays. Sara' birthday is close to Christmas. They planned on having a birthday party for Sara the following weekend."

"Yes, her birthday is December 9th" Leslie said. "I will never forget that date."

"She must have had friends then to invite to her birthday party" Alex added.

"The guest list for the party were all adults...family connections and business associates. Not a single child on the list."

"Poor baby" Leslie said quietly.

"Anyway, while they were in the city, the housekeeper asked me to help her clean the house to get ready. Afterall, it is a big house, and this was an important event. I was in the Nick's office cleaning the furniture.

He is a very neat and organized person. There was a pair of scissors on his desk. I opened the top drawer to put them away and I saw a small white ban with writing on it. My curiosity got to me, so I took it out and read the band. The writing was very small and hard to read. It said, 'Baby Sara, Daughter of Leslie Sherwood' and the name of the hospital and the birth date, December 9."

"They stole my baby" Leslie cried out and started to weep. It was as if she realized it for the first time and all the emotions flowed out.

Rebecca leaned over and put her arm around Leslie and held her while she wept. After a few minutes, Leslie pulled away and looked at Alex. "What do we do now? We can't let her stay there."

"What did you do with the wrist band?" Alex asked.

"I put it back in the desk. If I had taken it, it would have been missed. It is probably still there. At that point I decided I had to find you what was going on and I started my search. I spend the next six months getting and verifying information about Sara. I got information from old newspapers. There wasn't much, but enough for me to know that the baby in the papers is the same baby that I was taking care of. Your name was never mentioned but one newspaper article talked about a baby missing from the hospital in December. It also mentioned the name of the hospital. It did not take much to conclude that the missing baby was Sara.

"If you suspected this in December why did it six months to contact us?" Alex asked.

I had to be very careful in my investigation so could only work on it for short periods of time. I felt I was being watched. There are cameras all over the house. Then I had to come to grips whether this was right or not to get involved. How would this affect Sara? I went back and forth as to whether I should continue and look for you. Sara had to be my first concern, which was probably the main reason it took me a while to contact you. I had to be sure."

"Leslie's name was never mentioned in the newspaper so how did you connect her to Sara?" Alex asked

"Remember, her name was on the wrist band. I contacted the hospital and through many calls talking to different people I found out that a baby had been kidnapped from the hospital and her date of birth was the same as Sara's. And with your name on the wrist band, it was easy to determine that the baby was yours."

"Do you have any other evidence how Sara came to live there." Alex asked.

"I have no evidence other than the wrist band, which is a good start. Remember, when I told you that Nick and Maria were very happy about getting a baby through a surrogate and then toward the end there was a change in their demur. They were sad and then angry. I think the surrogate changed her mind and refused to give up the baby or something happened to the baby. I believe then that that the two of them came up with a plan to kidnap a baby."

"But kidnapping a baby? That is going to the extreme" Alex added.

"You forget how powerful the grandfather is. He kept asking when the baby will come home. Maria didn't want to disappoint her dad, and I think Nick was afraid of him. So I believe they decided to get a baby another way. The easiest way was to steal one. I have no idea how they ended up in Connecticut. But one day they came home with a baby and told everyone that the surrogate delivered their child. Everyone was happy, especially the grandfather. It was as if the baby were his child rather than his granddaughter."

"Do you think that he knew the baby was stolen from a hospital?" Alex asked.

"I don't think so. I think that only Nick and Maria knew."

"My daughter" Leslie said.

"Yes. Now I had to decide whether to contact you. Afterall, I had to think of what was best for Sara. Then something happened that convince me.

"I'm so glad that you contacted me" Leslie replied.

"Can I ask about her father? Is he in the picture? I assume you are not the father Alex."

"I was raped when I was 17 and Sara is the result of that rape. The guy was never found. I don't believe in abortions and I couldn't raise her on my own. I was still in high school. I decided that it would be best for Sara to be raised with a normal family. At the time. I thought that was the right decision. I'm not so sure now."

"That had to be terrible decision to have to make at that age...at any age."

Leslie grabbed Rebecca's hand again. "Thank you for doing this."

"I'm doing this for Sara. She needs a real home with her real mom."

"There is one other thing" Alex stated. "You keep saying that the grandfather is a very powerful man. But you never mentioned his name. Is there a reason."

Rebecca looked straight at Alex. "Yes, there is a reason. You know him."

"I know him" Alex asked.

"In fact, you both know him."

"We do?" Leslie remarked.

"Yes Leslie, you do. I was so surprised and shocked when I also learned that you worked at the same place as Sara's grandfather. The grandfather is Tony Gianti. It was then I decided I had to contact you. I could not leave Sara in this home and I didn't want her to be an orphan."

Chapter 29

"*T*ony Gianti!" is all Alex could say. "The guy in jail?"

"Yes, one and the same."

"Alex, we can't let Sara stay there" Leslie said,

"Yes…you can't leave that child in that home any longer" Rebecca added.

"Is she in danger? Are they hurting her?" is all Leslie could ask as she stared at Rebecca.

"No, nothing like that. But I don't think she is happy. Also, her grandfather is gone, and her parents kidnapped her. They will be discovered, and Sara would be alone. I can't let that happen to her.

"What does Sara know about her birth? Alex asked.

"I'm not sure what she knows. But several times she has asked me if she were adopted. I also heard her ask her parent the same question. Their answer was always 'no, you're not adopted' and then they walked away or changed the subject."

"That is a strange question for a child to ask" Leslie said.

"Your daughter is a very bright child. She has asked me the same question. She mentioned that she does not look like anyone in the family. At first, I just told her she was not adopted. It was only recently that I changed my answer."

"What did you tell her?"

"When I found out that she was stolen I felt she needed to know that she has a real mom. Afterall, with her grandfather in jail and her father and mother criminals she may end up alone. So, we had a talk and in doing so I told her she was adopted. But I also told her that she must never tell her parents that she knows. I know she never has said anything to them."

"How did she respond when you told her that she was adopted?" Leslie asked.

"No emotions at first. Then she asked. 'Is my mom looking for me?'"

"I assured her that her mom was looking for her and has been looking for a very long time. And eventually she will find you. With that she smiled and gave me a big hug. I only hoped that I was right and you would be looking for her."

"Alex, I have to see her" Leslie said. Then to Rebecca, "You have to help me see my daughter."

"Leslie, that house is dangerous. You can't go there" Alex responded.

"I don't care about me. I must make sure that Sara is okay. She must tell me herself. Alex please?"

"What would you say to her?"

"I don't know. Please, Rebeca can you help?"

"I know this is important to you. As I said, eventually, someone might figure this all out and I don't want Sara hurt and put into foster care. And I did promise that her mother would find her."

"Foster care? That never dawned on me"

"It has been on my mind since I found out she was kidnapped. Another reason I had to find you. Especially after Mr. Gianti was arrested. It is just a matter of time before Nick and Maria are found out. I had decided if it did happen, I would take Sara to live with me until her real mom was found."

"Please Alex?" Leslie asked.

"Alex, it is time for Sara to meet her mom. I promised her." Rebecca responded, looking straight at Alex.

Alex looked at Leslie and then back at Rebecca.

"Okay. How do we do this then? Any ideas?"

"Nick and Maria are going to a fund-raising dinner tonight. They are leaving about 5:30. You come by the house then. I will leave the front gate open. If it is closed when you get here it means they are still here."

"Okay."

"I better go, I don't want to be away too long."

They watched Rebecca leave and then looked at each other.

"Thank you, Alex. I have to do this."

"What are you going to say when you meet her? Have you thought about that? You need to look at this from the point of Sara. She is only ten years. How is she going to react?"

"I don't know what I am going to say. I'm hoping something will come to me then. I just have to make sure she is happy and safe."

"I totally understand. I don't know how you are feeling, but I know this is important to you and therefore it is important to me. Also, I have to make sure that you are safe."

"Alex, you have been my knight in shining armor from the beginning. This would never have happened without you."

"A knight...when do I get my reward."

"Don't worry, you will get it."

"We have a couple of hours before we can go. So, any suggestions how to fill them?"

"I don't want to sit here. The time would go by so slowly."

Alex took out his iPhone and checked for 'things to do' in Sag Harbor.

"Here we go. There is a Whaling and Historical Museum on Main Street. This is not far from here and it will pass the time."

"Good idea. Let's go" Leslie said sliding out of the booth and heading to the front door.

Alex paid the bill and followed her.

They spent the next couple of hours exploring the Whaling Museum and the other historical buildings on Main Street. The Whaling Museum was housed in a beautiful old colonial mansion. It displayed artifacts of items made from whale bones. There was a short informative movie that showed the lives of sailors on whaling ships. Across the street was the Public Library, also housed in a colonial building. Main Street was a tree lined street, exactly what you would expect in a Long Island community. After viewing artifacts in the museum, they walked along the street looking at the architecture of the houses and buildings on main street. At the same time, they both kept checking their watch.

At five-forty-five they passed through the open gate of the mansion at 18 Widow Coopers. Leslie watched the front door from the time they entered the property until the car stopped in front, hoping to get a close look at her daughter for the first time.

"I'm scared" Leslie said turning to Alex. "All of a sudden it is so real."

Alex grabbed her hand. "Let's sit here a few minutes to calm down. Take some deep breaths."

"What do I say. What do I do?"

"I think it best we let Rebecca take control of the situation. Listen to her and follower her lead. She knows Sara better than anyone and will know how to handle it."

"You're right Alex. Let her take control."

"If I feel that you are going in a direction that will frighten Sara, I will grab your hand. Is that okay with you?"

"Yes, please do."

"So, are you ready."

"Yes, I'm ready."

Alex got out and moved around to the passenger side of the car to open the door for her but she was already out of the car. Just then the front door of the house opened, and Rebecca appear in the doorway.

"Come on in. We've been waiting for you."

Alex grabbed Leslie's hand and they entered the large house. Rebecca turned to the right and they walked down a hallway to what appeared to be a family room or party room. The room was wood paneled with high ceilings. One wall was all windows and doors looking onto a swimming pool in the back yard. In the distance, there was a small guest house with all the lights on, just as Rebecca described it.

Alex felt Leslie stop as they entered the room, her hand squeezed his. Her eyes were focused on a young girl sitting on the sofa, hands folded in her lap. Anyone looking at her could see that she was Leslie's daughter. The same deep mahogany color hair that hung to her shoulders and matched the color of her eyes. Leslie just stood there looking at the child.

"Sara, I want you to meet Leslie and Alex, some friends of mine. They live in New York City" Rebecca said looking at Sara.

"How do you do Sara? It is so good to meet you" Alex said, trying to break the silence.

Sara just sat there, looking at Alex and then turning to look at Leslie.

Leslie let loose of Alex's hand and slowly moved over to the sofa and sat next to Sara, never taking her eyes off her.

"It is so good to meet you. Rebecca told us wonderful things about you. She said you are ten years old. You have a very nice house here."

"It belongs to my grandfather. He is not here right now. He is in jail. They said he did some very bad things."

"I'm sorry to hear that."

"You look like me."

"Yes, I noticed we have the same color of hair. But a lot of people have this color."

"Where do you go to school?" Alex asked trying to change the subject.

"I don't go to school. Mrs. Davidson teaches me here at home.

"Would you like to go to a real school, or do you like to go to school at home?"

"Grandpa says schools are dangerous."

Sara looked back at Leslie.

"Are you my real mom?"

Chapter 30

*L*eslie just sat there looking a Sara. She then turned to Rebecca not knowing what to say.

"Why do you ask that Sara?" Rebecca asked.

"She looks just like me" pointing to Leslie. "And you said that someday my real mom would come get me."

"You already have a mom and dad" Alex added.

"But they aren't nice to me. My real mom would be nice."

"What do you mean that your mom and dad are not nice to you" Leslie asked, a look of fear on her face.

"They won't let me go to school or have any friends. I have no one to play with."

"But you have this beautiful house and I'm sure that you have lots of toys here."

"I don't think it is nice. I have no one to play with."

"When Rebecca takes me to the store, I see lots of kids playing in the park and I never get to do that. My real mom would take me to the park."

"I'm sure Rebecca takes you to the park."

"She did once but when we got home my grandfather got mad at her. He said she was never to take me there again. I don't know why he got mad. But we never went to the park again."

"I'm sorry Sara" Rebecca said. "I wanted to take you to the park again, but your parents wouldn't let me. They were just looking out for your safety."

"But you would be there. I would be safe. I don't understand."

"Someday you will understand. When you are grown up."

"What did you do when you were in the park?" Alex asked.

"I liked the swing. There was a girl in the swing next to me and we were both laughing. It was so much fun."

"Swings can be a lot of fun, especially when someone pushes you" Alex added.

"What do you like to do when you are in the house?" Leslie asked. "You have a big yard to play in. Do you have a swing here?"

"Yes, grandfather put a swim up for me in the backyard. It is hanging from a tree. But it is not fun to swing along."

"I see you also have a swimming pool in the back yard. That must a lot of fun" Leslie continued.

"I like to go in the swimming pool. But I can't go in unless someone is there with me. But sometimes I go in when no one is around."

"You shouldn't go in by yourself. That could be dangerous. You might get hurt and no one would be there to help you" Leslie said

"Do you have a swimming pool where you live?

"No, I don't. I don't live in a big house like this and I don't have a yard. But I live very close to a park. And there are swings in my park too."

"Why are you sad?"

"Why do you think I am sad?

"Your eyes are all wet."

"I am not sad. Those of tears of happiness. Sometimes when a person is very happy tears will form in their eyes. Right now, I am very happy."

"Why are you happy?"

"Because I was able to meet you. That makes me happy"

"I am happy to meet you too."

"Would it be okay if I gave you a hug?" Leslie asked softly.

"Okay."

Leslie moved closer to Sara and gave he a big hug, holding on longer than usual.

"Thank you" Leslie said as she let go.

"I like hugs."

"A girl as pretty as you. I'm sure you get a lot of hugs."

"No, I don't. Except Rebecca and grandfather. But he is not here now. Rebecca gives me lots of hugs."

"That is because you are so huggable" Rebecca said with a smile.

"I bet your real mom is looking for you right now. It is very hard to find someone when you don't know where to look" Alex stated. "But I know that someday she will find you." Alex looked at Leslie after he said that, thinking that may he should not have daid anything. There was no reaction from Leslie. She just continued to looking at Sara through tearing eyes.

"I hope she finds me. I don't want her to be sad."

"But you have a mom and dad now" Leslie added. "And I'm sure they love you very much."

"But I still want my real mom."

"I hope you find her" Alex added. "She will be a lucky person to have a daughter like you."

"Sara, please come over here. I need to talk to you" Rebecca said.

Sara got up from the sofa and moved over to the chair where Rebecca was sitting and stood in front of her. Rebecca took both of Sara hands in hers and looked squarely into her eyes.

"Sweetie, you know I love you very much. And I would never do anything to hurt you and make you unhappy."

"You never make me unhappy. I always have fun with you."

"You know that I will always tell you the truth. I will never tell you a lie. Remember I did promise that someday your mom will find you and once she finds you, you will have to decide if you want to live with her or stay here and live in this house. That is a very big decision."

"I hope she finds me."

"I have been looking for your real mom for you. Do you understand what I am saying?"

"Yes, you want to find my real mom just like I want to find her. She must be unhappy without me and I don't want her to be sad."

"You are a very special little girl. I want to tell you something now that will make you happy."

"What?"

"Leslie is your real mom. She has been looking for you for a long time".

Sara turned and looked at Leslie and said, "I knew it."

Tears were running down Leslies cheeks. Sara walked over to Leslie and said, "Don't be sad."

"I'm not, I'm so happy right now. These are happy tears."

Leslie slowly put out her arms and Sara walked right into them.

"I love you Sara. I have always loved you. I'm sorry it took so long to find you."

Just then they heard a car door slam. Rebecca left the room and headed down the hall. She came back quickly with a look of fear on her face.

"Nick and Maria are home early. She looked at Leslie and Alex.

There was a look of panic on Leslie's face.

"They will be coming in here. Please follow my lead." She then turned to Sara.

"Please don't tell your mom and dad about Leslie. Can you do that for me? Just like the game we play 'mum's the word'?"

With that they heard the front door open and close and soon after that the sound of high heels clicking on the marble floor and getting louder as they came down the hall. Maria stepped into the room with Nick behind her.

"We are home early. I was not feeling well so we decided to leave early and come home. Oh, I see you have company."

Nick stood there a while looking at Leslie and then Alex.

"I need to go put the car in the garage." He then turned and left as Maria stood there looking at Alex and Leslie.

"I just wanted to say goodnight before I headed to bed. And who may I ask are you two."

"These are friends of mine from the city. They are in the same book club with me. We are reading a Russian Novel and they stopped by to discuss it."

"You know I don't like visitors in the house when I'm not here."

"I'm sorry" Alex said. "It is my fault. We just stopped by unannounced. And Rebecca was gracious enough to invite us in to discuss our current assignment. It will not happen again I promise you. Again, I apologize."

"It is just that Sara is not used to strangers and I don't want to upset her."

"Everyone looked at Sara who was sitting quietly on a chair next to Rebecca.

"Is everything okay Sara?" Maria asked. "Do you know these people?"

Everyone held their breath.

"No. They came to see Rebecca."

"Maybe we should leave them alone."

Just then Nick appeared again at the door and looked straight at Alex. "Good to see you again, Alex."

Alex turned to Nick. "What do you mean again?"

"Maria, take Sara and Rebecca to another room now" Nick said, authority in his voice.

Maria took Sara by the hand and left the room, Rebecca behind them. Sara turned and looked back at Leslie as she left.

"Again, I apologize for stopping in without calling ahead. But I didn't know I would be close by. We will leave now. And again, I apologize, and it won't happen again" Alex said as he stood up.

"I know it won't happen again and no need to be in a hurry. This makes it all so easy. I have someone I want you to meet."

Just then Tony Neuman stepped up behind Nick holding a gun at his side.

"Just like Nick, I'm glad to see you again Alex. And you too Leslie."

Chapter 31

*L*eslie grabbed Alex's arm.

"Let's all sit down and become reacquainted" Tony said, waving the gun at Alex and pointing to the sofa. Leslie and Alex sat down on the sofa, Leslie still holding on to Alex's arm. Tony and Nick sat in chairs facing them.

"You looked puzzled or is that fear I see on your face Alex" Tony said with a snicker.

"I have to say I'm not surprised. You are in the right company" Alex remarked, staring at Nick, and trying not to show any fear.

Aren't you the brave one" Tony remarked. "Let's just see how long that will last."

Alex continued to stare at Nick and then back a Tony. He could feel Leslie's hand squeezing his arm tighter.

"Oh, where are my manners. You haven't met Nick yet" Tony said motioning at Nick with the gun.

"Nick, meet Alex. The guy responsible for putting your father in law in jail."

Nick just sat there motionless, staring at Alex and Leslie with no expression on his face.

"Alex, this is Nick. I think he dislikes you almost as much as I do."

"I can't say I'm happy to meet you" Alex replied.

Nick continued to start at Alex, no expression on his face, but there was hate in his eyes.

Tony got up from his chair, walked over to Alex, grabbed him by his hair and bent his head back, pushing the nozzle of the gun under his chin. Leslie gasped.

Alex could see hate on Tony's face as he stared up at him.

"If it had not been for you, I'd be sitting on a beach in South America" Tony say, pulling Alex's heard further back.

"I suggest you leave now and catch your plane before something stops your trip again" Alex responded.

"I have some unfinished business before I leave. I want to hear you beg for your life. I have thought about this moment with every minute I sat in that jail cell."

"You did this to yourself, Tony. I didn't kill three people. You did that on your own."

"I was hoping for two more before I left the country…you and this pretty lady" he responded, removing the gun from under Alex's chin and waving it toward Leslie. "Loyal Brianna caught on and warned you. That bitch got what she deserved."

Tony released Alex's head and moved back to the chair, the gun at his side. Alex never took his eyes off Tony.

"Now we need to figure out what to do with you two." Tony turned to Nick. Nick looked at him and just shrugged his shoulders.

Tony turned back to Alex.

"I bet you are wondering why I am here. Am I right?"

"Well it did cross my mind."

"I kind of grew up in this house." Tony continued. "My mother worked for Mr. Gianti. She would bring me to work with her each day. There were two children in the family, Maria who just left and her older brother Mario. I had someone to play with. Mario and I became good friends. The Giantis treated me like family. Mrs. Gianti always called me her second son. She wanted me to feel like I as a member of the family, but I knew I wasn't. I had to go home to our one-bedroom apartment over a Chinese restaurant every night. A reminder of who I really was. To this day I can't stand the smell of soy sauce."

"It sounds like your mom took good care of you. She made sure you had a place to go each day, friends, and a roof over your head. What more did you need?"

"You don't understand do you. You probably had everything you wanted growing up. I didn't. All my clothes were from a second-hand store. I slept on a pull-out sofa."

"You had a home, a family who loved you, food on the table and a mom who took care of you. You were far better off than a lot of kids."

"The kids I went to school with all came from rich families. They made fun of me. One day I came to school with a shirt that one of the kids in my class has given to the thrift store. Everyone laughed at me. They treated me as a second-class citizen. Since I lived on the 'other side of the tracks' as they say, I liked coming here. I got use to the good things in life and swore that I would never struggle like my mom did."

"It appears you found what you were missing in this home. So, what happened to change you into something else?" Alex responded, not sure if it was the right thing to say. He waited for a response.

"I was only a guest here. None of this was mine. Each day here reminded me of where I came from."

"I'm sorry you had to go through that. But we all had our struggles growing up."

Tony continue to talk about growing up. It was as if he was talking to himself, trying to convince himself he was justified in what he did.

"After high school Mario went off to college. I tried college but it wasn't for me. Mr. Gianti even financed it. I left college and took a job with a trucking company. I hated it. It didn't pay enough for me to live like this, so I quit. However, the short time I was there, I met some colorful people...people who showed me how to get rich quickly. They helped me in my future endeavors, so to say. The future looked good. Then my mom developed cancer and only lived four months after the diagnosis. I was an orphan at the age of 23. Again, Mr. Gianti came to my rescue and took me in."

"Sounds like he was a good father figure for you." Alex added. "So, what happened to turn you into what you became?"

"You mean...a killer?" Tony said with snicker.

"I guess that is what I mean."

"Mr. Gianti took me in and treated me as one of his own. He loved me. Something no one else every gave me. I would have don't anything for him."

"From what you said, you mother loved you very much."

Silence.

"She didn't give me anything."

"So, because Mr. Gianti had money, he loved you and your own mother, who sacrificed everything for you, didn't love you? That is a strange definition of love. Now that you have money, why not just pack up, head south, and live the life you want?"

"You don't get it do you. You put the only person who loved me in jail."

"I'm sorry, but he broke the law?" Alex responded. I didn't put him in jail. He did that to himself. I guess I can assume you got the 'consulting job' at Sterling through Mr. Gianti."

"Mr. Gianti discussed his work with me. He told me that he was worried about his job and the new product that they were going to start selling. The company was in financial trouble and the product would save the company and his job. He said there was something wrong with the product, but they would find a solution while the product was being sold. He also stated that a few people in the company were starting to question it."

"It was a bad product. It would destroy our environment and put lives in danger in future generations."

"Let them worry about that. Not my problem. I told Mr. Gianti that I would help him. He told me that Dawn Manning had come to him and told him that the product was bad, and she was getting evidence and was there to ask him to stop its introduction. He told me that he would lose a bonus of about a million dollars if the product was bad and sales delayed. We couldn't let that happen."

"So, you eliminated Dawn for him? Did Mr. Gianti ask you to do that?"

"No, but I know he appreciated it. He put fifty thousand dollars in an account for me for doing that. Then when Peter Hudson came to him with the same concern, he asked me to help him out again. Another fifty thousand in my account."

"You didn't think that was wrong?"

"One hundred thousand dollars or two people's lives? That was an easy decision."

"Then I entered the picture."

"Everything was fine, and we thought it was all behind us. Then you joined the company. Since you took Peter's place, I was asked to follow you to make sure Peter didn't leave you anything. I followed you when you met with his wife and saw her give you some papers. Now you two were added to the list."

"Why didn't Mr. Gianti just help fix the product and delay the selling of the product."

"That is a stupid question. We would lose our bonus."

"Oh, I see." Alex noticed that Tony said 'we' rather than 'Mr. Gianti would lose his bonus."

"And I got a big bonus too" Tony said with snicker.

Alex remembered the fifty-thousand-dollar payment for each murder. When he was reviewing the documents that Brianna had given him, he had found funds transferred from a Miami bank to an offshore account.

"Oh, I forgot" Tony continued. "Remember Rob, who also worked at Sterling? The 'all American boy'? He was the younger brother of one of the guys I worked with at trucking company. I convinced Mr. Gianti to bring him into Sterling and help keep an eye on things."

"Why are you telling me all this?" Alex asked.

"I thought that with your inquisitive nature you would want to know. If you want me to stop, I will, and we can get on to the good part of my plan."

"What was Rob's role in all of this?"

"He was brought in to keep an eye on people coming and going and talking to Mr. Gianti. We had to make sure there was no one else asking questions. One day he accidentally saw Brianna copying classified documents. Rob followed her when she delivered the documents to you. You probably already guessed, but he was the one driving the car that killed her. One more person eliminated.

Working with Leslies father, Alex had uncovered a payment of fifty thousand dollars transferred to an offshore account for Rob.

"Then there was only you left, and I would have enough money to leave New York and head to South America for the beach and sunshine" Tony continued. "Rob would take care of Cindy. I must tell you that Sterling Chemicals is not the first company where I used my 'special skills' and probably won't be the last."

"How does Sara play in all of this?" Leslie asked.

All eyes turned to Leslie. She had been sitting there very quiet.

"That's another whole story."

"I want to hear it" Leslie said with a firm voice.

"Okay, it is a good story to tell. Mario was killed in an automobile accident his second year of college. Mr. Gianti was devastated. He turned to me for the son he lost. I also became a stand-in-brother for Maria. She had a wild wicked side to her, and he wanted me to keep an eye on her. On one of her party nights she met Nick. That led to dating and eventually marriage.

"So now you had a father figure and a sister. Everything you wanted. So, what happened?" Tony asked.

"I still felt like the kid from the other side of the track. I had to show everyone that I could make it on my own. I had to prove to everyone that I was someone. I had to make a lot of money."

"Money doesn't buy happiness" Leslie said.

"But it puts a good down payment on it" Tony said.

"So why not go to work and make some money?" Alex asked.

"That wasn't fast enough."

"So, what did you do then? Act as a 'consultant' at some other company?" Alex asked, trying to keep the conversation going, while looking for a way out of this situation.

"Mr. Gianti wanted a grandchild and pressured Maria into getting pregnant. But that didn't happen. She and Nick tried but it wasn't in the cards. So, Maria, Nick, and I we came up with a plan. We found a surrogate to carry the baby and Maria would pretend she was pregnant. She would go to the hospital when the baby was born and come home with a child claiming she gave birth, and everyone would be happy. Mr. Gianti would have his grandchild."

"I assume that something happened that there was no child" Alex stated.

"Damn mother decided to keep the baby. Nick didn't know what to do. Mr. Gianti wanted a grandchild. Maria and Nick came to me and asked me to help then get a baby. They were willing to pay big to get one."

"So, you just decided to steal a baby."

"That was a quick and easy way to get a baby. Maria had gone through the nine months of pretending to be pregnant, so we had to produce a child. Her father was waiting for his grandchild. We had to do something. So, I found a hospital in Connecticut and the rest is history."

"Didn't you even think about how the parents of the child would feel?" Leslie asked.

"The baby was being born into a single parent home. I know what I went through and did not want that on any child. This child would be brought up in a good home not wanting for anything. And I got fifty thousand dollars for one day of work. Everyone wins." Tony said looking at Leslie.

"Did Mr. Gianti approve of your method of getting him a grandchild?" Alex asked.

"He never knew" Tony said.

"Who actually took my baby from the hospital" Leslie asked.

"I did" Tony said. "I didn't realize you were the mother until after you started working at Sterling. When I saw the name on your cube it did not take me long to determine that you were the mother. Of course, I could not tell Mr. Gianti, but I was able to keep an eye on you for Nick and Maria. I had to make sure you did not find out about the baby. Only Nick and Maria knew how the baby came to live here."

"You are a monster" Leslie said. "Taking a baby away from her mother."

"What's the big deal. You were going to give it up anyway."

"That is no reason to steal a baby. Do you know what you put me through? And my parents?" Leslie said with anger in her voice.

"Ask me if I care about your feelings."

"You are an evil person" Leslie responded under her breath.

Alex turned to Nick. "Do you really want to be part of this and what Tony plans?"

"He has no choice" Tony answered.

"What do you mean he has no choice?"

"Well, I got the baby for him, so he owes me. Nick helped me escape from jail. He has also been with me several times as I followed you two since my escape. We were hoping to get a chance to 'finish the job' but never got you two alone. You have made that so easy now... you came to me."

"I try to please" Alex replied trying to keep the conversation going so he could figure something out.

"By the way, how did you put it all together?"

Leslie looked at Alex. She didn't want to say that Rebecca put them on the right track and get her in trouble.

"Um. I happened to find the name of the couple who were going to adopt the baby. I had agreed to put it up for adoption. I was told that the baby died in the hospital. When I ran across the couple's name recently, I wanted to meet them and tell them how sorry I was. They told me that the baby was kidnapped. So, I contacted the police and got copies of all their documents."

"But how did that lead you to this house."

Alex jumped in, making up a story as he went along.

"We didn't find anything in the documents we got from the police, so we quit looking. By coincidence we are both in an online book review club. The same club that Rebecca is part of. We are currently discussing the book **The Diamond Chariot**. It is a mystery novel in two parts by a Russian author, Boris Akunin. The main character is an investigator named Erast Fandorin. It takes place during the Russian-Japanese war."

That book had been an assigned reading in a class Alex took in college. It made a big impression on him, so he remembered the names. He was sure that neither Tony nor Nick had heard about it, let alone read it. Using the book club as his cover, removed Rebecca from the scheme.

"So how did that get you here?" Nick asked.

Alex continued, making things up as he went along.

"As I said, we belong to an on-line book club where members can text back and forth with their thoughts and ideas. We found Rebecca's thoughts and ideas very compelling. She told me that if I were ever on Long Island and in the area to stop by so we could discuss our thoughts about the writer's approach to the mystery. We called this afternoon and said that we were on Long Island and wanted to stop by and meet and discuss the two books. So, here we are."

"You expect us to believe that?" Nick asked.

"Believe what you want, it is the truth."

"Even if that is the reason, it is the last book you will ever read" Tony said as he waved the gun at Alex. "You put me in jail."

"You put yourself in jail. You were responsible for the deaths of three people. People who will never grow old or enjoy seeing their children grow up. Do you ever think about them and what you took from them?"

"I just did my job. Now it is time to finish the last phase of my job before I head to South America."

Chapter 32

*L*eslie grabbed Alex's arm.

"Some job" Alex said under his breath. "So, how did you come to be here now when we are here?"

"That's another story. I needed some place to hide out once I escaped from that jail. I have been living in the guest house out back. This is a big piece of property, so I was not noticed by anyone coming and going. Even Rebecca didn't know I was here."

"I'm glad you were comfortable, for now."

"You are funny. Once I get rid of you two, I am off to South America and I can't be touched. Sitting around all day basking in the sun drinking margaritas. The question now is to how and where to get rid of you two? Any ideas Nick?"

Leslie squeezed Alex's hand harder and let out a slight whim.

Nick has been sitting quietly the entire time just watching Tony. He wished he could be as cool as Tony. While sitting here listening, he realized he was deeper in this scheme then he ever wanted to be. Right now, he was sweating under the collar and just wanted to get out of here. But he knew that if Tony was around, and this matter wasn't settled, he would be under Tony's control. The only way to be free of Tony and this situation is to get him to South America.

"Why not just let us go and head to South American" Alex said. "The longer you wait the greater the chances you will be caught. Just get on that plane and leave and let us all get on with our own lives. Getting rid of me won't change anything" Alex said.

"It's the principle, buddy boy…you sent me to jail."

"I didn't send you to jail. Your actions put you there."

"So, what do you think we should do with these two?" Tony asked, turning his attention back to Nick.

"The family owns 25 acres of secluded land in the Poconos. We could go there, and you do what you need to do. Just leave me out of it. I've never killed anyone before."

"It is so easy. Just pull the trigger" Tony said raising the gun and putting it at Nick and pretending to pull the trigger.

Nick's sat up straight in the chair, his eyes wide open and sweat appearing on his brow.

"Don't worry Nick, I'll put the trigger. I just need you to dig the holes."

Leslie grabbed Alex's arm and started to cry. "Can I say goodbye to Sara?"

"You mean, say goodbye to your daughter?' Tony remarked laughingly.

"You Bastard!" Leslie screamed.

"Enough" Tony said. "Let's go." He pointed the gun at Alex. "Time for us to go on a trip."

Alex slowly got up from the sofa without a plan in his head. He took Leslie hand.

Just then the doorbell rang.

"Nick, go answer the door and get rid of them. You two, sit back down and not a word or I'll shoot you here."

Alex and Leslie sat down as Nick heading to the front door. Tony sat in the chair across from the sofa, the gun still pointing at Alex.

They all listened to the conversation at the door after Nick open the front door. They heard talking but they were so far away that they could not understand what was being said.

Silence....

"Everything okay Nick" Tony yelled down the hall.

Silence...

Just then Nick appear in the doorway of the room, a look of fear on his face. He just stood there. Tony dropped his arm down, the gun pointing to the floor.

"Glad you got rid of them. Now we can take care of our business" Tony said.

Just then Nick was pushed into the room. Behind him stood two men holding guns aimed at Tony.

"Drop the gun Mr. Neuman" one of the men said.

A look of fear crossed Tony's face.

Just then they all heard the doors leading to the pool area open and two men walked in with guns pointed at Tony.

"I repeat, drop the gun Mr. Neuman. There is no way out. You raise you gun one inch and I'll fire, and you will hit the ground before your gun does."

Slowly Tony released the hold on the gun, and it fell to the floor. Instantly one of policemen by the open door to the pool moved over to Tony, kicked the gun to the side and put handcuffs on him. Nick was pushed into the room and hand cuffed.

One of the policemen moved over to Alex. "Are you two all right?"

"Yes, we are" Alex responded. But how did you know?"

"Easily" a voice said coming from the hall doorway "We just followed you."

Everyone looked toward the door. There stood Lisa Fisher from the district attorney's office.

"Once you told me that you thought Mr. Neuman was back in New York we decided to follow you. We knew you would reject so we didn't ask."

"How long have you been following us?" Leslie asked.

"We were with you when you went to Connecticut, and the print store, and then here" Lisa continued. "When the police saw you stop outside this home earlier today, they called me. I came right out. When we saw you go into the house, we thought something might be wrong. The police sat outside until I was able to get a search warrant. I just got it about fifteen minutes ago. Good thing someone left the front gate open."

"I'm so glad you didn't listen to me when I said we didn't need an escort. Thank you."

"You are welcome. Okay guys, take these guys away? And don't forget the wife."

Tony and Nick were led away.

"Are you all right?" Lisa asked.

"All I can say is Thank You again" Alex said.

"Sara, what about Sara? Leslie asked, grabbing Alex arm.

"She is fine Lisa. Let's go see her. Rebecca mentioned that she is your daughter. You will have to explain that to me" Lisa commented.

"I will. Just let me see her and make sure she is all right."

"Come with me."

They all left the room where they have been held captive and walked down the hallway toward the front entrance. As they passed the front door they stopped and watched Tony, Nick, and Maria, all in hand cuffs, getting into separate police cars. Lisa then led them into a large sitting room. There on the sofa sat Rebecca and Sara.

Leslie ran over to Sara knelt and grabbed her. "Are you okay Sara? Are you hurt'"

"I'm fine. Rebecca took care of me."

"Thank you, Rebecca" Leslie said, still holding on to Sara.

"Guess I'll have to find a new job" Rebecca said. No one here to work for.

Leslie stood up.

"I have tears of happiness in my eyes" Sara said, "just like you."

Sara took Leslie's hand, looking up at her.

"Let's go home mommy. Can we go to a park tomorrow?"

Everyone in the room had tears in their eyes.

Leslie turned to Alex and grabbed his hand.

"First thing in the morning, we will all go to the park" she said, looking at Sara, and then at Alex.

CPSIA information can be obtained
at www.ICGtesting.com
Printed in the USA
BVHW081406091120
592845BV00014B/1490